Ghost Writer

A Paranormal Cozy Mystery

Dina Marie

ISBN: 978-1-964858-02-9 (ebook)

ISBN: 978-1-964858-03-6 (paperback)

Book cover design by Elizabeth Mackey

Acknowledgments

I'd like to thank Tina Greene-Bevington, Nathan Bay, Karen Sinclair, Jenna McGrath, Brian Fagan, Chris Carter, Jennie Evenson, Shanee Edwards, Danielle Wolff, and, of course, my editor Joan Martinelli.

For Mom

Chapter 1

I STEPPED BACK TO admire the new beige valance at the top of the window overlooking Salem's tree-lined street. A far cry from the decrepit, old shades that had been hanging there for years. Together with the new blinds, the valance looked stylish and bathed the living room in glorious morning sunlight. Unfortunately, the light also highlighted the dust, worn furnishings, and everything else that needed updating, but I reminded myself that renovating an old house and opening a bed-and-breakfast took time. Lots of attention and careful planning. Just like my escape from my awful marriage and journey to find the *me* I was supposed to be. Whoever that was. I moved the ladder to the next window to hang another valance.

"Are you certain you don't wish for me to undertake that task for you?" William asked. He pulled down on the jacket of his Union soldier uniform.

He had been hovering all morning. I knew that ghosts were *supposed* to hover, but today it seemed to be more than usual. William's normally gray pallor was somewhat darker, his piercing pale blue eyes filled with uncertainty. Probably thought a military soldier should be the one doing the manly things around the house, like renovation or repair. *You can take the man out of the 1800s …*

"No, I've got it, William, but thank you. Remember, I like doing things myself."

"And you say that most women do, likewise?" he asked, befuddled.

"Yes." I smiled. "Very much so. But, you know, you could hold the ladder for me, if you like. It's a bit rickety."

"Yes, I can attend to that," he said, the gray of his face brightening.

Together, we hung the rest of the window treatments. I was proud of myself for being able to decipher the poorly drawn illustrations. It was nice to brush out the cobwebs of my brain and get it working again.

"What's the next course of action?" William asked.

"Well, I've got the electrician coming later today, the plumber tomorrow, and if all goes well, I'll have the new appliances here in a few weeks." The thought of cooking my own food made me giddy. Joe had never wanted anything that veered much beyond meat and potatoes, which meant that meat and potatoes were all I had to eat for eight years. I thought of all the cookbooks I could buy. The dishes I could try. The longtime favorites I could make, like my dad's famous salmon meatballs. My mouth was watering already.

"Will you be lodging at the hotel again this night?" he asked.

"I think so. But I'll be staying here soon, once there's hot water. I'm still shivering from the cold bath I had to take with Boy earlier this year." I laughed. "Seems like forever ago, doesn't it?"

I glanced down at Boy, who was sitting in front of the fireplace, tearing apart what was left of my blond wig. Since I had given it to him, he had practically abandoned all his other toys. It was his favorite thing. I would have thrown it out, but it made him so happy. And he deserved to be happy. We both did. William, too. I knew some unsettled matter was keeping William here, haunting this old house—an underlying sadness always seemed to plague him—but if I could figure out why Beckett Miller was murdered, then I could most certainly figure out why William was here, too. At least, I hoped I could.

"Oh, I have a surprise," I said.

"Oh?" William asked.

I hurried into the dining room and reached into my backpack on the chair. I took out the framed document and held it up for William.

He studied it. "Is that …?"

"Yes. It's the list of ground rules you made when we first met. I had it framed. I thought we could hang it near the front door for guests to see." I held it against the wall.

William began to read. "Rule Number One: No callers are allowed beyond the primary dwelling quarters."

"I know that one was meant for me," I said with a smile, "but now it's pertinent to the guests of the bed-and-breakfast, right? This is their space, and that'll be our space." I pointed to the secret rooms on the upper floor. They weren't so secret anymore, but I liked calling them that.

"Indeed." William kept reading. "Rule Number Two: Nought shall be rearranged. The furnishings, whether exterior or within, are to abide in their present state."

"That works, too, right? We can't have guests tearing up the joint."

He furrowed his brow, maybe a bit baffled by my use of the word *joint*. "Rule Number Three: We treat one another with the utmost respect."

"That's still my favorite."

He glanced at the fourth rule in my handwriting, squeezed in at the bottom in pencil. "Rule Number Four: We don't talk about the past."

I watched him closely. "That one still stands, right? I mean, I don't mind erasing it. That's why I wrote it in pencil."

"The Witch House is right down here, I think," the man with them said, pointing down the road. "We'll head there first before lunch."

"But, Mommy!" The little boy grabbed his mother's cheeks. "I saw, there's a ghost there!"

As the trio passed Mr. Wiggins and me, the mom placed the little boy on the sidewalk and said, "Kids have such imaginations."

They're also pretty perceptive.

"Are you looking for the Witch House?" Mr. Wiggins asked.

"Yes," the man said. "Do you know where it is?"

"Sure do."

As Mr. Wiggins gave the man and woman directions, I bent down to talk to the little boy.

"You saw a ghost in there?" I asked.

He nodded his head.

"Tall? Wearing a funny-looking suit?"

He nodded again.

I leaned toward him. "I believe you," I whispered.

He smiled.

"Thanks so much," the father said to Mr. Wiggins. As the couple continued walking, the little boy turned around. I gave him a thumbs up. He gave one back.

"What are you up to today, Ms. Clara?" Mr. Wiggins asked.

"Well, I've got the electrician stopping by this afternoon. The plumber, tomorrow. Thank you again for the recommendations." I looked up at the side of the house and touched the brickwork. "I was thinking of getting the exterior of the building cleaned as well." It was strange to think how little money I had had when I first arrived in Salem. Only the cash in my pocket. But with Joe's death, and New York's inheritance laws, I had suddenly come into a substantial amount. I liked to think I deserved every penny after what I had put up with for eight years. Plus, I had vowed that whatever I had inherited would be used for good. And restoring this beautiful home—for William, for me, for Salem—was at the top of my list.

"A cleaning is a good idea." Wiggins pointed to the front of his house. "Got mine done a few years back. It's held up well. I'll get you the nice young man's phone number who did it for me."

"What's that?" I asked, pointing to a plaque on the side of his house.

"Oh, that's from the historical society. I'm sure your house is listed in the historic home database as well. You can get one, too. All you have to do is put in an application." He pointed down the road. "The historical society is located not too far from the Witch House that that lovely young couple was heading to. I'm sure the society members can tell you more about it."

A car pulled up, and Mr. Wiggins waved to the driver. "Well, my ride is here." He walked carefully toward a handsome young man, probably about eighteen, who got out of the driver's seat. "Mathis, no need to bother yourself and get out of the car."

"No bother at all, GG!"

"He calls me GG," Wiggins said to me with pride. "Mathis, this here is my new neighbor, Clara."

"Happy to meet you, Clara." Mathis shook my hand. "Thank you for looking after my great-grandfather."

"Now, who's to say who is looking after whom?" Mr. Wiggins chuckled.

I couldn't argue with that.

As Mr. Wiggins and his great-grandson drove away, I looked again at the plaque on the side of Wiggins's house. It made the home look so official. Like it was part of history. I looked at my house with its grimy brickface. William deserved to be a part of history, too. And it would be a cool thing for passersby to see on the building.

I walked back into the house.

"Boy, I'll be back in a little while. I'm going to take a walk to the historical society. Take care of things for me, okay? You're in charge."

Bark!

Ghost Cat appeared from somewhere in the kitchen and glanced at me.

"Yes, you too," I said. "You're second in command."

When Boy spotted her, he chased after her as she walked through the wall that separated the main room from the living room. I noticed Ghost Cat made a habit of walking through walls just to confuse Boy, although he didn't seem to mind. He barked a few times when he couldn't follow her and then went charging into the living room through the open doorway.

I smiled at the unlikely pet siblings as I grabbed my purse. One of life's surprises. I looked forward to many more.

Chapter 2

THE SALEM HISTORICAL SOCIETY was in a quaint, colonial-style building with a red brick exterior. No surprises there, as much of Salem was colonial brick red. Inside were all kinds of brochures and flyers associated with the town's history, mostly about the infamous witch trials. I browsed through them and took note of some events and lectures taking place in the next month. Then I approached a heavyset woman sitting at a desk. Her nametag read *Mavis*.

"Can I help you?" Mavis wiped the powder of a donut from her mouth with a napkin. The napkin on her desk read *The Haunted Cookie*.

"Yes, I own one of the historic buildings here in Salem. I'm interested in getting one of those little plaques for the exterior of my home."

"Well, first we have to find out whether your home is, indeed, historic." Mavis raised her eyebrows.

"I'm pretty sure it is."

Mavis gave me a look like she'd heard that before. "Well, we'll just have to find out, won't we?" She pulled her swivel chair toward a computer and pushed the last of the donut into her mouth, crumpling up the wax paper around it into a ball. "Which property is this for?" She glanced up at me for the first time. Her eyes widened. "Wait a minute, are you Clara Kelly?"

"Yes," I said, surprised. "You know me?"

Mavis tossed her trash into a wastebasket. "I know *of* you, if that's what you mean. Saw your picture on Bev's Insta feed. I never forget a face."

"Bev?"

"Beverly Lanford, who works over at Derby's. We've been in a knitting circle together for nearly nine years, and, boy, I've heard all about you." She glanced proudly at a knitted coaster on her desk that was under a coffee cup.

Ah, Beverly. The town gossip. How could I have been surprised that I made her Instagram feed? I was probably the talk of Salem these past few months.

"So, you're the gal who moved into town a while back," Mavis said. "Husband fell down the stairs. A terrible accident, I'm sure." She looked at me skeptically.

"Yes, it was," I said, trying to keep things short and sweet. *Nothing to see here!*

"I already know your address. You moved into the old Kensington House property, right?"

"Yes!" I said excitedly. How amazing that William's house was already known as a historic building. Kensington House. And it had a cool name to boot!

Only Mavis didn't seem to think it was so cool. "Are you sure you want to do that, put a plaque on the side of your building for all to see, considering the history?"

"What do you mean?"

"Well, I don't know. If I lived there, I'm not sure I'd want to publicize the person the building was built for."

"I don't understand."

"Not much to understand." Mavis rolled her eyes. "William Kensington was a traitor to his country. Now I ain't no social media influencer like Beverly, but I know for sure I wouldn't want *that* on my Instagram feed."

Traitor? William? "That's impossible. William Kensington couldn't have been a traitor. You must be thinking of someone else."

Mavis sat back and crossed her arms. "Well now, don't I just love it when newcomers come to the area thinking they know Salemanders' business better than we do."

"Salemanders?"

"Salem residents," Mavis explained as if that were even a word. "William Kensington's life is a historical record. No fake news here." She looked me up and down. "But if you're still insistent on ordering one—a plaque, that is—there's an online form you can fill out."

"Thanks," I said absently and left the building before Mavis could say anything else.

Outside, the air was cool and crisp, but my face still felt warm from Mavis's accusation. There was no way William could have been a traitor to his country. I didn't know him long, but I knew him well enough.

Or did I?

Yes, he had saved me from Joe, but William was in Salem haunting that house for some reason. Could it have been the guilt associated with being a traitor?

I had the urge to run back home and ask William directly, but I wasn't sure how far that would get me. He certainly hadn't been forthcoming with anything from his past, other than how he had come about his ghostly prowess. Was that why he was so keen on instituting Ground Rule Number Four, *Don't talk about the past*?

A crowd had gathered across the street in front of a storefront that read Ye Olde Salem Book Shoppe. My heart fluttered. A bookshop only a few blocks from my house? A bookworm's dream. I thought of William. There might be some books about the local history of Salem that mentioned him. I looked at my watch. I had plenty of time before the electrician's appointment. It was worth a visit.

Chapter 3

I crossed the street and excused my way through several women taking photos of a small sign that read *Book Signing Today: Best-selling Author Marlena Ryder, 12 p.m. to 2 p.m.* Inside the bookstore, at the back, seats had been arranged in front of a small stage. A woman with long blond hair and short bangs was standing on the stage holding a book while patrons were oohing and ahhing around her. I approached the register.

"Hi, I'm looking for books on Salem's history. Do you carry any?"

A dude in a denim button-down shirt gave me an apologetic face. "Well, you've come to the right place. But, unfortunately, at the wrong time. We're having an author event at the moment, and our local history section has been moved to accommodate that event. If you come back later today, we'll have all the shelves back in place. Ask for me. I'll be working. Name's Aaron."

A pair of women entered, squealed at the sight of the blond woman on stage, and hurried to seats in the front.

"Who's the author?" I asked.

"Well, you must be from out of town," Aaron said with a smile. "Marlena Ryder is a celebrity around here. A best-selling thriller author. Her book's been a number one *New York Times* bestseller for three weeks in a row."

"Wow, that's exciting."

"And pretty unbelievable for a debut author," Aaron said. "Marlena grew up around here. Has been coming to this bookstore for years, I'm told. Always wanting to be a writer. She's been trying and trying." He smiled. "We're all so proud of her. You may want to stick around. She's got a great story to tell." He held up the book. "And you can buy it here, if you like."

I shrugged. "I'm not much of a thriller reader." I had enough thrills going on in my *real* life. "But maybe I'll stick around for a bit."

I managed to find a seat in the back as a woman with large, round glasses got up on stage. "All right, everyone, please take your seats. We have a very exciting event taking place, and I know you all would like to get right to it." The murmuring began to die down. A woman sitting beside me, who had purchased three copies of the author's thriller book, could barely sit still. Her hand, which was resting on top of the stack, had an interesting geometric tattoo that reminded me of the pendant around my neck, my dad's gift to me. I reached for it and rubbed it. *I missed him.*

The woman on stage continued speaking. "For those of you who don't know me, I'm Sadie Smith, the owner of Ye Olde Salem Book Shoppe, and I'm honored to be bringing you one of Salem's very own." The packed house began to clap. "Marlena Ryder needs no introduction. Suffice it to say, she has been a longtime patron of this store, and we're thrilled she finally got her big break and, with all her success, has made time for us. So without further ado, welcome, Marlena!"

The audience stood, cheering and clapping. Some women upfront even appeared to be crying. It was as if Taylor Swift had just been announced.

"Thank you so much," Marlena cooed, moving the blond bangs from her eyes and looking out into the audience. "I see so many friends here and fellow book club readers and writers from my old workshop. Thank you for all your support. As most of you know, I grew up not far from here, in a pretty blue house on Carlton Street. And if you're like me, I know you all have been to so many book signings here at Sadie's lovely bookshop." There was another round of applause, and Sadie took a short bow. "So, if it's okay with you, I'd like to answer your questions first before my reading. I'm sure you have all these questions bubbling up—I know I did when I used to come to see my favorite authors here—so let's, as they say in the thriller genre, cut to the chase." The audience laughed. "Does anyone have any questions they would like to ask me?"

Dozens of hands shot up. I felt self-conscious about not having any questions. Like I was back in school and had forgotten to do my homework.

"Let's start with you, Kendall, in the front," the author said.

A young girl stood up and pulled down on her baggy UMass shirt, looking nervous. "Thank you, Marlena. May I call you Marlena?"

"Yes, of course."

Kendall covered her mouth as if to refrain from screaming in delight. "I'm just so excited to be here."

"Why, thank you so much!" Marlena said.

"Well," Kendall said, "my question is, why did you want to become a writer?"

"Great question! I've always wanted to be a writer. To tell stories. To entertain. I think it's because my momma didn't like me saying much when I was a kid, didn't like me telling my side of things." The audience laughed. "Now, I get to tell stories the way I want. And I feel blessed to be able to do that for a living."

"Thank you," Kendall said and sat down. "You're so inspiring."

Sadie pointed to the back. "You, in the purple. Do you have a question?"

The woman in purple was sitting in the row in front of me. She stood up, and I realized it was Alice from The Haunted Cookie. She still had her long dark hair in a ponytail and looked to be wearing an apron. Like she had come during her lunch break.

"Was getting a book published hard?" she asked in a tiny voice.

"I'm sorry, can you say that again?" Sadie asked. "Alice, is that you?"

"Yes, ma'am." Alice cleared her throat as the woman who had been sitting beside me picked up her things and moved to a seat in the second row that had been vacated. "I was wondering if it was hard to get your book published." A lot of heads bobbed up and down in the audience as if wanting to know the answer.

"It was at first," Marlena said. "As my fellow workshop writers in attendance can attest, I'd been pitching agents and publishers for many years. I took on editing jobs and coached other authors to make ends meet. The publishing industry can be brutal. And soul-sucking. I could have given up long ago. But I didn't. I was determined. My advice to you is to never give up, never take no for an answer. Great things can come when you believe in yourself."

Marlena's response, while enthusiastic, seemed a bit cliché and canned. Like something she read on a meme from social media. But it seemed to satisfy Alice, who nodded and returned to her seat.

"Excuse me," a tap on my shoulder, "is this seat taken?"

I looked up and into the greenest pair of eyes.

"Sebastian, hi," I said, embarrassed.

"May I sit?" he asked, motioning to the empty chair beside me.

"Sure."

He sat, his cologne wafting under my nostrils. "I almost didn't recognize you." He glanced at my long red hair.

"Yeah." I grabbed a piece of my hair. "Red."

"It suits you." He smiled. "No more wig?"

I thought of Boy ripping it apart. "I found a better use for it."

"Are you back in town for a while?"

"You mean you didn't hear?"

"Hear what?" he looked at me, his green eyes sparkling.

Apparently, Beverly's gossip network had not reached The Pampered Pup. "Never mind. Yes, I'm back in town for a while. A long while. I moved here."

"Really?" he asked, his eyes widening. "That's great news."

I could feel my lips curving into a smile, but I stopped them. If I could have put a clothespin on my nose to keep from smelling Sebastian's cologne, I would have done that, too. I needed to focus on me for a while and not Salem's kind, cute pet groomer. No flirting. No dating. No kissing. *But how long has it been since you had a real kiss with a real man?* No. No. No. Stop thinking. I had things to do. A business to open. I changed the subject. "Are you familiar with her?" I pointed to the stage. "Marlena Ryder?"

"Sure, most Salem residents are. It was a big deal here when she got a publisher for her book. Made all the papers."

The audience laughed. Something funny must have been said, but I missed it because I was trying not to look at Sebastian's green eyes.

"Do you have a question?" Sadie was pointing to the right side of the audience. "You in the blue-striped shirt?"

The blond woman who had been sitting next to me stood up. "How long did it take you to write your book?"

"A wonderful question!" Marlena smiled. "It's funny," she glanced around the audience, "I've always struggled with novel writing. But this book came easy to me. I guess it took me a while to find the right idea. It only took a few months. Thank you so much for your question."

"A question in the back!" Sadie said.

A well-dressed man stood up. He was wearing a suit, as if he had stopped by after an important meeting. Other than Sebastian, he was the only man there. "What is your favorite part of being a writer?" he asked.

"That's easy!" Marlena motioned grandly with her arms. "Meeting readers!"

Boy, this Marlena Ryder really knew how to work a crowd.

The audience applauded again as Sadie pointed to another reader who asked a question. Then Sadie began snapping photos of the audience as the author answered that question and about a half dozen more before Sadie announced the Q&A portion of the event was over.

"Marlena," Sadie said, "will you read a bit for us from your best-selling book?"

"I'd be happy to. Thank you all for the wonderful questions." Marlena opened to a bookmarked page in her novel. "It's always hard to pick a place to read from in a thriller. You never want to give too much away."

The audience laughed yet again. I was beginning to think the author could have told us that she set fire to the town square and everyone in the audience would cheer her on.

"I figured," Marlena continued, "I'd start at the beginning. Chapter One ..." She cleared her throat and began reading, her voice in a dramatic, lower register. "Melanie awoke with a start. Someone was watching her. She didn't know how she knew, but she knew. The air had changed. She sat up in bed, her eyes darting around the room. 'Is someone there?' she asked. No answer. But then again, she didn't expect one."

"Oooh, this is scary," Sebastian whispered to me.

I laughed. "Have you read her books?"

"I'm not really a thriller type of guy. Don't see a reason to go out of my way to scare myself and make me even more paranoid than I am."

"Same."

"I read a lot of nonfiction," he whispered. "How-tos and all that."

"Yeah, I think I will be, too. I don't know the first thing about house maintenance. Or running a bed-and-breakfast."

"Are you turning your home into a B&B? That's great."

"Yeah, and I'm ready to learn. Ready to do things for myself—by myself."

I stiffened. Ugh. I hope I hadn't said too much. I didn't want Sebastian asking what I meant by all that. Luckily, he didn't.

"That's the spirit. Although you don't always *have* to do things by yourself. You can ask for help from your friends."

His green eyes twinkled, and that seemed to be that. I wanted to tell him I had no friends, really. Well, besides a kind but sad ghost living with me whom at least one person in Salem believed to be a traitor. But I didn't want to get into all that. Sebastian had no idea about my past—or my present—and I didn't want to tell him. Was I embarrassed? Scared? Private? Maybe all those things.

The audience clapped loudly, and Sadie stood up. "Well, if that doesn't wet our whistle, I don't know what will! I'm sure we could keep Marlena here for hours, and she's been so gracious. Another round of applause."

Really? *Another* round of applause. By this time, the audience members would have developed callouses. As soon as people rose from their seats, two elderly women made a beeline for a velvet-roped area at the side of the store where the book signing would probably commence.

"We'll be starting the book signing in about ten minutes," Sadie said. "I see some of you are already in line. Is that you, Teresa and Kaitlyn? Wonderful! If you don't already have Marlena's thriller novel, *The Secrets We Keep*, it's available for purchase. Aaron, wave!"

Aaron, the young man I had been talking with, was standing at the register and holding the thriller novel up in the air.

"So go ahead and pick up your copy," Sadie said. "Another thank you to Marlena Ryder!"

More clapping from the disbanded audience as Sebastian leaned over. "How's Boy?"

"You remembered his name."

"How could I not? That might just be the greatest, non-creative pet name I've ever heard."

Sebastian was so cute. *No! No, he isn't. Abort! Abort!* "He's great. He's back at the house right now. Actually, he's way due for another grooming. The last one he had was the one you gave him. He smelled so great. I loved the shampoo you used."

"Great, I'd love to see him again. I have your number, right? I can text you some openings I have."

"Oh, um ... my number changed." No need to tell him the first number I gave him was for a burner phone I tossed.

"What's your new number?"

I told him, and he entered it into his phone. "I'll send you a text, so you have mine. And I'll get back to you soon with some appointment times." He looked at his watch. "I'd better go. I have a grooming appointment in fifteen minutes."

"Sounds like fun."

"Oh, you haven't had fun until you tried to clip the nails of a nearly hundred-pound labradoodle. See you soon."

As Sebastian made his way out of the store, Aaron came toward me. He began picking up and folding the chairs. "I see you're still here," he said.

"Yeah, got caught up, I guess."

"Well, if you've got a few more minutes, we should have the shelves back in place soon. You can take a look at those local history books you were asking about."

"Great." I stood up, and he reached for my chair. "Do you need help with that?"

"No, that's okay," he said. "Chair maintenance is only part of the reason I get paid the big bucks around here."

I stepped aside and waited for Aaron to clear the floor. At the side of the store, the line for the book signing was getting longer, snaking along the wall and dipping outside. Luckily, it was a nice day, or there would be some pretty soggy thriller readers out there.

Aaron began pulling several shelves on wheels into the store and arranged them into aisles. He locked the wheels and pointed to one of the shelving units. I walked over and took a look. There were rows and rows of books on Salem's history.

"Wow, you weren't kidding," I said. "This is quite the selection."

"Well, when you're a big tourist town," Aaron said, "you gotta give 'em what they want. By the way, you haven't seen Sadie, have you?"

"The woman who was on stage with the author?"

"Yeah, I don't see her around. And she's not answering my texts. Someone has a question about summer hours. That's okay. Thanks anyway. Let me know if you need help finding anything."

"Okay, thanks." I watched him walk back to the front of the store. This seemed like such a cool place. If I hadn't majored in hospitality and tourism management in college, English would have been my second choice.

I browsed through the assortment of titles, picking up books related to the late 1800s and some of the earlier citizens of Salem. I checked a few indexes but couldn't find anything about a William Kensington.

I didn't know how long I had been browsing, but when I looked up, the line for the book signing hadn't moved. Teresa and Kaitlyn were still standing at the front, only they appeared less enthusiastic than they were before.

Aaron was nearby, adjusting one of the genre signs. "What's going on?" I asked him. "Why hasn't the signing started?"

"Marlena has been in the ladies' room." He shrugged. "Did you find Sadie?"

He checked his phone. "She hasn't texted me back." He took a look around the store. "Oh, there she is." He pointed.

Sadie was standing near a desk where presumably the author would be sitting for her signing. She was adjusting a bouquet of flowers and several Sharpies. She looked at her watch and walked over to the restroom at the back of the bookshop. She knocked. "Marlena? Marlena, we're ready to get started."

No response.

Sadie looked at Aaron, who shrugged. Sadie knocked again.

"Marlena, dear, are you okay?"

No answer. By now, everyone standing in line—everyone in the entire store—was looking at the bathroom door.

Sadie knocked again. "Marlena?"

Nothing.

Then Sadie reluctantly put her hand on the restroom's doorknob, turning it a little. When it gave, she slowly turned it all the way.

"Marlena," Sadie said, "I'm so sorry to disturb you. I just want to make sure—"

She never finished her sentence. Instead, she let out a blood-curdling scream, covering her mouth as the door swung open and the bloodied body of Marlena Ryder lay slumped on the bathroom floor, her throat slit and a copy of her book, *The Secrets We Keep*, open on top of her.

Chapter 4

Officer Carl Callahan stood near the bathroom door, shaking his head. His partner, Officer Fred Manning, was talking to Sadie, who was blowing her nose, her face red and puffy. Manning had already been through the store, asking me and everyone else if we had seen anything, but no one had. Which seemed crazy. After being married to Joe, though, I knew what could occur when everybody was around and no one was watching.

I waited in line as, one by one, the bookstore patrons were allowed to leave the store after providing Manning with their contact information. Most of them were crying. When I got to Manning, I gave him my name and phone number.

"Clara Kelly?" he said, eyeing me.

"Yes. We've met before, Officer Manning. You came to my house a few months ago. When my husband—"

"I remember. That's right." He glanced at my hair and then at Officer Callahan, who had finished talking with Sadie. As Callahan and Sadie parted ways, a lone figure was left behind, standing near the bathroom. A woman. Gray. *All* gray.

My heart began to race.

Oh no.

Before I could look away, her gray eyes met mine.

"Hey!" she shouted. "You can see me?!"

Not again.

Officer Callahan was standing in front of me, cocking his head. "Have we met?"

I barely heard what he said as the ghost of Marlena Ryder came running next to him, shouting at me. "I was murdered! I was murdered! Are you just going to stand there?!"

"This is Clara Kelly," Officer Manning said to Callahan while I stood there trying, unsuccessfully, not to look at Marlena Ryder's ghost.

Callahan glanced at my red hair. "New hairstyle, I see."

"Yes." *It's actually old, but no need to split hairs.*

Callahan looked toward the back of the store, where Marlena Ryder's body was covered with a black tarp. He probably thought that's what I was looking at. Little did he know. "Why is it you seem to make a habit of being around dead people, Clara Kelly?"

He didn't know the half of it. Marlena Ryder's ghost was standing right next to him. "Just bad luck, I guess," I said.

"You've given your statement to my partner, Mrs. Kelly?"

Was he always going to call me *Mrs.*? "I really didn't see anything. I had been browsing some of the local history books when the bookstore owner discovered the body. But I gave Officer Manning my contact info if you need me for any reason."

"Very well. We'll be in touch, Mrs. Kelly, so stay in town."

"Oh, I'm in the process of becoming a resident of Salem, so I'm not going anywhere."

Callahan eyed me strangely. "Moving into the house where your husband died? Doesn't that seem a little ... morbid?"

"Trying to make better memories, I guess." I shrugged. "Trying not to run away from things anymore."

That seemed to satisfy him. For the moment. He nodded and went off to talk to a pair of EMTs who were inputting information into a tablet.

I nodded at Officer Manning and made my way to the store's exit, trying to ignore the gray figure following me. *Why was there always a gray figure following me?*

Outside, a large crowd had gathered. Some were crying. Others were gawking, holding phones into the air, and trying to get a glimpse of the gruesome crime that had taken place in their neighborhood bookshop.

"Wait up!" Marlena's ghost said. "I know you can see me. You looked right at me."

I kept walking.

"I'm guessing if you can see me, then you can hear me, too."

I ignored her. Maybe if she thought she had been mistaken, she would go away.

"Lady! I'm talking to you!"

I crossed the street, wondering if I could somehow lose her, when Marlena shouted, "Watch out for that car!"

I stopped suddenly in the middle of the crosswalk and looked around. There were no cars anywhere.

"See?" she said. "I told you that you could hear me."

Ugh. I couldn't believe I fell for that. I got to the other side of the street and turned to face her. "What do you want?"

"What do you think I want?" she said, exasperated. "I want my life back."

I knew she did. Beckett had wanted his life back, too. "I'm sorry. There's nothing I can—"

"Who are you talking to?"

Taylor Hampton, the snarky reporter from the *Salem Chronicle*, was standing next to me, looking at me strangely.

I reached into my back pocket and pulled out my phone. "Do you mind? I'm on a call."

Taylor looked at the dark phone screen. "I think you've been disconnected."

I looked at my phone. *What now, genius?* "Are you still there?" I said into my phone screen, bringing it close to my face. "Hello? William?!" That was the only name I could think of. The only friend I had.

"Well, I think William hung up on you. Or you him," Taylor said with a snicker. "A little advice. Try holding your phone in your hand when you're using it. I think you'll have more success that way." He laughed at his own brilliance and headed toward Ye Olde Salem Book Shoppe.

"Beckett was right," I muttered. "He really is such a jerk." I put the phone to my ear.

"I really don't care," Marlena said. "Someone *killed* me and …"

Don't say it. Don't say it.

"You have to help me find out who that person is."

She said it.

"What do you mean?" I kept walking. "Don't you know already?"

"No! Whoever it was must have been waiting for me in the bathroom when I went in there."

I stopped walking. "The person was already in there?"

"Yes, I guess he or she was behind the door when I opened it. When I closed it, someone covered my mouth and then slit my throat. Next thing I know, I'm standing inside the bathroom with my body on the floor. If Sadie Smith hadn't opened the door, I don't know how long I would have been in there."

Marlena Ryder hadn't yet figured out how to walk through walls. She would with time. And practice. *How weird that I know these things!*

"You have to go back there and tell Officer Callahan what happened," Marlena said. "He won't listen to me."

"He can't hear you."

"But *you* can. Tell him what I told you."

"How? There would be no way for me to know what happened to you unless *I* was the one in the bathroom."

Marlena thought about it and took a step back.

"Um, I *wasn't* the one in the bathroom," I said. "I don't even know you. Why would I kill you?"

"I see your point."

I looked at my watch. "Listen, I don't mean to be rude, but I have an appointment this afternoon and have to get home."

"But what are we going to—"

"There is no *we*. Listen, I've been here before. Don't ask. I can't help you." My phone buzzed in my hands, startling me. I looked at the text. The electrician was on his way? Already? Ugh. "I have to go. I'm sorry. You'll have to find somebody else."

I kept walking, but Marlena followed me. "I have nobody else."

I couldn't be the only one who saw ghosts, could I? I thought of the little boy who had seen William through my window. Obviously, he couldn't help Marlena. He could barely tie his shoes. But that meant others must be out there, right? *Somewhere.*

"You're my only hope, Mrs. Clara Kelly."

"I'm not a Mrs."

"You're not? But that officer—"

"It's a long story."

I quickened my pace. I could see my house a block away. Almost home! *I think I can, I think I can …*

"I'm so sorry," I said. "I've got to go. And I kind of have this policy that I don't allow ghosts in my home. I hope you understand."

By the time I got to my narrow driveway, I almost walked right into a car parked there. I expected to see the electrician waiting for me on my doorstep, but he wasn't. Someone else was.

Oh no. My sister-in-law, Allison.

And she didn't look happy.

Chapter 5

"Well, hello, Emily." Allison held up a key. "I see you changed the locks."

"Allison! Hi! What a surprise!" I found myself stepping in front of Marlena Ryder, not knowing if my sister-in-law was one of the lucky few who would be able to see and hear ghosts. I had a feeling she wouldn't be. Allison Turner barely noticed anything other than her own mirrored reflection.

"Well, are you going to let me in?" Allison gave a heavy sigh.

I really would rather not. "Of course."

I opened the door, and Boy greeted me excitedly.

"What the hell is that? A rat?" Allison asked.

"It's my dog," I said defensively and turned to Boy. "Sorry to be so late, buddy." I picked up his water and food bowls. I refilled both. "What are you doing here, Allison?"

"I should be asking you the same thing." Allison put her bag down on the dining table and started looking around. "This is *my* house, you know. At least, it should be. You have no right to it. I don't care what New York State's inheritance laws say." She stopped at the stairway and looked up. "So, this is where it happened, huh?"

I placed Boy's bowls down on the floor. "Yes. It was a terrible accident."

"Yeah, I read the police report, although I'm not so sure you think it was either terrible *or* an accident."

I studied Allison. For years, I had wondered whether she knew her brother, Joe, was an abusive husband. She and Joe were always close. If she did know—and it was very possible she did—she had done nothing about it. She had been no friend to me. I didn't trust her then. And I certainly didn't trust her now.

Allison began walking around, looking at the front windows. "Doing a little staging, I see."

"Staging?"

She pointed to the new blinds and valances. "For Rhonda, the realtor, I assume."

I shook my head. "No, I'm not selling. I've already been in touch with Rhonda. Actually, I fired her."

"Why did you do that?"

A lot of reasons. "I've decided to move here. To Salem. Living on Long Island, in the house that Joe and I shared, is just too ... hard." *Not the right word, but it was the word I was going with.*

"So, you move to the place where he died?" She gave another little huff.

Between Callahan and Allison, I realized this was going to be an issue for people. I had better get used to answering this question. "I'm moving to a new place, period. Trying to create better memories."

"My parents tried to reach you, but your number isn't working."

"That's weird," I said. "I got a new phone, but I sent them the new number. I'll text it to them again." We stood there, looking at one another. "Um, what can I do for you, Allison?"

"Well," she faced me, "to be blunt, I'm contesting the inheritance. Damn laws in this country. There's no way you should be getting all of Joe's properties. I told him he should have had a pre-nup. He always said he had things under control."

Oh, is that what he called domestic abuse? Control? "I'm sorry you feel that way. As I told your parents, they can have the house on Long Island and all the trusts and properties and whatever else there is. All I want is this house and some seed money to get me started." I also had my father's house on Long Island, although I hadn't gone back there yet. I dreaded how quiet it would be without him.

"Oh, how generous of you … How nice of you to give them the house my brother and I grew up in so that you can move here into this historic old house that has been in my family for more than a hundred years."

"Allison, you and I both know that Joe had no interest in this house. Neither do you or your parents. You rarely visited. You spend most of your time at the house in the Hamptons and in Cape Cod. Joe had been looking to sell. That's why he was working with Rhonda, right?" Well, that and *other* reasons. "I fell in love with this house the minute I got here and want to make it my own, turn it into a bed-and-breakfast, start again. I would hope that you would wish me well."

"Well, you hoped wrong. This house is my birthright." She came close to me and looked me in the eye. "And if you think I'm going to believe that my brother, Joe, a track star in college, fell down a staircase to his death, you've got another thing coming. There's more to this story. I *know* it." As she picked up her purse, Boy began to growl. "This isn't the last you've heard from me." She strode through the front door and right into Marlena Ryder's ghost, who was standing on the front steps.

At least I knew, for sure, that Allison couldn't see Marlena.

As Allison drove away, Marlena asked, "What was that about?"

"Don't ask."

"I tried coming into your house," Marlena said. "But I couldn't walk through the open front door for some reason."

"You can't. Not unless you're invited."

"So invite me," she said.

Boy, these ghosts can be pushy. Before I could tell her that I liked my privacy, a voice came from the end of my driveway.

"Clara Kelly?"

A man in baggy jeans with tools hanging from his belt was standing there.

"Yes. Come in!" I called, and the electrician made his way to the front door, also walking right through Marlena. "Basement door is that way." I pointed. When I turned back to Marlena, looking miserable and dejected, I was overcome with guilt. Ugh. "Listen, I have an appointment right now," I said. "But I'll meet you when it's done, okay? You know that bench right outside The Haunted Cookie?"

"Yeah. I know it."

"I'll see you there."

She nodded, looking a tad more hopeful. When she got to the sidewalk, a tour was walking by, and Marlena seemed to glance at every person, as if waiting to be noticed. I realized that Marlena Ryder was used to being the center of attention. Especially in Salem, Massachusetts, where she had readers practically swooning in her presence.

Being dead was bad enough for an adoration-craving best-selling author. Being invisible was far worse.

Chapter 6

I WAS STILL REELING from the price the electrician gave me as Boy pulled me down New Derby Street toward The Haunted Cookie. Tens of thousands of dollars? I told myself it would be worth the investment if I ever decided to sell the house since the old wiring wouldn't support modern tech demands. Apparently, old wiring also raised the risk of having a house fire. If I left things the way they were, Joe might have gotten his wish after all. The whole place could have burned down.

Marlena was standing near the bench, right outside The Haunted Cookie. Boy ran toward her, his tongue hanging out of his mouth. He loved being outside. When Marlena saw Boy coming, she took a step back as if afraid.

"He's friendly," I said. Not that it mattered. Boy would have run right through her.

"I'm not really a dog person," Marlena said.

I sat down on the bench and whipped out my phone. Boy sat next to my legs and looked around at all the people walking by, one of his favorite activities besides ripping apart my blond wig and chasing Ghost Cat around the house.

"I tried to sit on the bench," Marlena said, "but I couldn't."

"I know. It's going to take a while for you to figure out how to manipulate objects and things. Give it time."

"How do you know so much about all this? Are you some kind of psychic or spirit medium?"

"Nah, just sort of ghost *adjacent*." I thought of William. I hadn't seen him during the electrician's visit. He probably didn't want to be intrusive. I petted Boy's head. "I'm not sure I can help you, but I thought the right thing to do was to hear you out. What exactly happened?"

"You were at the book signing, right?"

"Yes, I was sitting in the back."

Marlena's eyes gazed off into the middle distance. "It really was a beautiful event. An event I had dreamed about. As Sadie said, I had been to her bookshop many times. As a kid. As an adult. I always wanted to be a writer. And to finally have a best-selling book and be able to stand there on stage where I had seen so many of my favorite authors speak? It was more than I could have asked for."

"You have a lot of fans."

She smiled. "It's been wonderful. The book signings. The *New York Times* bestseller list. Being selected for Jenna Bush Hager's book club. It's been everything I ever wanted." Her smile faded. "Until it was cut short."

"Why do you think someone wanted to hurt you?" It had to be personal. I found it hard to believe some depraved lunatic would decide to go to a book signing and use the bathroom without locking the door, and then murder the first person who walked in. Although stranger things had happened.

"How do *I* know? How do you know it wasn't random?"

"Well, I'm no private detective, but there were signs that either the person who did this knew you—or knew of you."

"What do you mean?"

"Well, first of all, your book. It was left open on your body. Almost like some kind of calling card or message."

"Maybe whoever did this just forgot to take it with them."

"That seems too sloppy. And that's the other thing. Your books were only available at the register. In order for the murderer to have a copy of it, he or she would have had to purchase it. Unless it was purchased somewhere else."

"You're right. If it was purchased in-store, maybe there's a credit card record."

"Or maybe they paid in cash. We don't know. All I'm saying is, whoever it was went out of their way to buy the book, here or somewhere, sit through the Q&A, and then during the activity between the Q&A and the book signing, get into the bathroom." I thought some more. "That's the other thing. How did the killer know you'd use the bathroom?"

Marlena's cheeks tinged red. "I usually do. I have a weak bladder." She shrugged. "Always have."

"Ah, so the killer must have known that!"

A woman walking past the bench glanced at me when I said the word *killer*. I pointed to my phone and smiled. *Nothing to see here. Just a woman talking to a ghost about her murder and pretending to talk on the phone.* "It's someone who knew your habits. This person may have been following you for quite some time and just waiting for the right opportunity."

Marlena gave a tiny shiver as she seemed to take that in. "You're making the whole thing sound a bit scary."

For a thriller author, Marlena Ryder didn't seem to have the stomach for violence. "You seemed to know quite a few people at the event," I said.

"Yes, I lived here for many years. I know a lot of people."

"Did I hear correctly that you were part of a writers' group in Salem?"

Marlena nodded. "Yes."

"Could it have been someone from the writers' group?"

"I find that hard to believe. They idolized me," Marlena said with a smile. "I mean, we've known each other for years. They're friends of mine."

"Well, jealousy can make you do crazy things. You used to be one of them, a struggling writer, and now here you are a best-selling author. I'm sure some of your colleagues may have been a little envious." But could that envy be enough to kill someone?

"I don't know." She shook her head. But then her face changed.

"What is it? Did you think of something?" I held the phone closer to my ear as two college students glanced at me as they passed.

"Well, there was this woman in my writers' group. Ronnie. She also writes thrillers—or, at least she used to write them. She always had the harshest criticism for my books. I could tell she never liked me."

"Was she there at the book signing?"

Marlena nodded. "Yeah, I'm sure not by choice. She was probably dragged there with the rest of the women in my group. From what I understand from some of the other writers, Ronnie had a couple of nibbles from literary agents, but they never panned out."

Marlena's lips curved into a smile just a tiny bit. I got a sense there was some competition there. "This Ronnie person lives in Salem?" I asked.

"Yeah, I don't know where. She used to work at Haute Chocolate part time. Tuesdays and Thursdays, I think. I'm not sure if she still does. That would be a great place for you to start."

"Me?" Boy put his paws on my legs, and I pulled him up. He circled a few times before plopping on my legs.

"Well, duh, *I* can't ask her anything."

"Sorry, but I can't get involved."

"You're already involved."

"I came here in good faith."

"You didn't have to."

She had a point, but I wasn't about to let her know that. I didn't have to meet her here. *Why did I?* Why did I feel compelled to hear Marlena out?

Marlena seemed to sense my ambivalence. "It'll only take a few minutes," she said.

"I have the plumber coming tomorrow." Even *I* thought that was a lame excuse.

"Do you really want me hanging outside your house for the rest of eternity?"

Ugh. How do I get myself into these predicaments? "All right. I'm not making any promises. I'll go tomorrow morning. Tomorrow's Thursday, right? If this Ronnie person is there, I'll talk to her for a bit."

"Great. I'll meet you there when it opens."

I put Boy on the ground and stood. "What will you do until then? Do you have a place you can go?"

"I don't know. I sold my house when I got my book deal."

"Wow, you didn't waste any time."

"Listen," she crossed her arms, "I've lived here long enough and paid my dues. It was time for greener pastures. I have a place in New York City. High rise near the Hudson River."

"Sounds expensive."

"The sunsets are worth it. Beats this small town. Salem is no New York."

Hmmm ... Off-stage Marlena didn't seem quite as nice as on-stage Marlena. Somehow all that gratitude and love for her fellow Salemanders—as Mavis called them—seemed to have died with her body in the bathroom.

"I'll find someplace to go," she said. "Maybe I'll head to the library. See if they have my book in stock. I'll see you at Haute Chocolate. Don't be late."

Great, I thought as I watched her go. Just what I needed. Another bossy ghost. And another murder to solve.

Chapter 7

I WAITED IN FRONT of Haute Chocolate, sipping the last of my coffee. *Where the heck is Marlena?* For a ghost who demanded I be punctual, she was running late. I wondered if she got stuck in the library. I didn't know what time it opened, but it was very possible she was waiting for someone to open the door for her, unless she had figured out how to walk through walls.

I looked at my watch. I would have to get things moving without her. I had to get back for the plumber. I wondered how much *that* was going to cost me. Joe had money, but I had a feeling his sister wanted to keep most of it. Suddenly, there seemed to be an urgency to get my bed-and-breakfast up and running. And here I was wasting time playing sleuth. Again.

The smell of chocolate hit me as soon as I walked in, reminding me of the delectable little treats I purchased the last time I was here. I looked for the owner, Sissy, but behind the counter was a dark-haired forty-something woman with tortoiseshell glasses. She looked up at me.

"Hi, can I help you?" she asked with a smile. Her name tag read *Ronnie*.

Target identified.

"We're running a sale today to commemorate Chocolate Day on these items here." Ronnie pointed to a section of the display case. "Buy five and get one free."

"There's a Chocolate Day?"

"Yep. There are lots of them. National Chocolate Day. International Chocolate Day. National Milk Chocolate Day. National White Chocolate Day. You get the idea."

Ronnie seemed friendly enough. I didn't know what I was expecting. A bloody knife in her hand?

"Okay," I said, "I'll look around, thank you."

"My name is Ronnie. If you need help, just let me know."

Perfect. Ronnie was here. Ready and willing. Now I just needed a reason to talk to her about Marlena Ryder. As I glanced at all the differently colored and shaped chocolates, nothing was coming to mind. All I could think about was National Chocolate Day and which five items I was going to buy to get a freebie. Then I saw a book sitting on the counter just beside Ronnie. Bingo. "Oh, are you reading that?" I asked.

"Yeah." She held up the book titled *How to Become a Best-selling Author: The Secrets the Publishing Industry Doesn't Want You to Know*. "I picked it up the other day. Honestly, there's nothing in here I didn't already know."

"Are you a writer?"

"Yeah. Trying to find a literary agent. Not having much luck."

"Hang in there. I'm sure you'll get there." I paused intentionally, making it look like the next thing I was about to say wasn't planned at all. "Oh, my gosh, I was at the bookshop yesterday and saw what happened to that author. Did you know her?"

I watched Ronnie carefully for signs of anxiety or duplicity—anything that seemed out of the ordinary—relying on the skills I developed spending eight anxious years with my duplicitous husband. But there was nothing.

"Yes, that was just terrible." Ronnie placed the book back on the counter. "I *did* know Marlena. We attended the same writers' workshop for years."

"Oh, I'm sorry."

"We weren't really *friends*, per se. But we had been writing together and sharing our stories over the years. I felt like I knew her well."

So far, so good. Keep her talking. "Well, that must have been some writers' workshop to produce a best-selling author!"

A pained look appeared on Ronnie's face, and she got quiet. So much for keeping her talking.

"I'm sorry," I said. "I don't mean to talk about it. This must be painful."

"Are you a writer, too?" she asked.

"Me? No. I'm lucky I can write my shopping list." I smiled. "What is your genre?"

"I write historical fiction. I used to write thrillers, but I changed genres."

"Historical fiction. Wow, that must require a lot of research."

She nodded. "It can." Ronnie got quiet again.

"Sorry. I'll just browse the chocolate." I went to step away when Ronnie spoke.

"No, I'm the one who should be sorry. I have to admit, I was so jealous of Marlena when she got that book deal. And so ... well, angry. Now, I just feel guilty."

Anger? Jealousy? Those were two motives for murder. Guilt? Was that a confession? Where the heck was Marlena? It suddenly occurred to me that I might be standing alone in a small space with a murderer. I slowly took several steps away from her.

"Sorry. I didn't mean to scare you away," Ronnie said with a smile. "It's just all so ... you know, *raw.*"

"No, I get it." *Get me out of here.* "I just remembered, though, I have an appointment with my plumber. I'll have to come back later and check out some of the on-sale chocolate."

"All right," Ronnie said. "I'll be here. See you soon."

I hurried out of the store and took a breath. Well, *that went well. I keep telling these ghosts I'm no detective.* Why don't they believe me? I reached under my T-shirt, pulled out the compass pendant my father gave me, and rubbed it to calm myself down.

As I began walking home, I saw Officer Callahan across the street talking to someone. He didn't look too happy. But when did he ever? The thought occurred to me that I should mention something to him about Ronnie being a suspect. He should be checking out that lead. He was getting paid for this. I wasn't. Where was Marlena?

I walked toward him, but as I got closer, I saw he was talking to Taylor from the *Salem Chronicle*. No wonder Callahan was in a bad mood. I made a quick right, but it was too late. Callahan turned and saw me. "Clara Kelly. You're up bright and early today."

"Good morning, Officer Callahan. Yes, I was just in Haute Chocolate."

"You seem to pop up everywhere, don't you?" Taylor was eyeing me warily. "Where's your phone? In your pocket?" He smirked.

"I was just ending my conversation with Mr. Hampton," Callahan said.

"But I have more questions about the murder," Taylor said.

"Maybe another time. I have a few things I need to discuss with Mrs. Kelly."

Ugh. It's *Ms.* Kelly. But at this point, it felt like it had become too late to correct him.

Taylor looked annoyed, but he put his notebook away. "I'll be in touch," he said to Callahan and then gave me a dismissive look and walked away.

"Thanks for the save," Callahan said to me. "That Taylor Hampton can be quite a nuisance." He raised his neatly trimmed eyebrows. "So, you must love chocolate. Visiting Sissy already? It's not even ten o'clock in the morning."

"Um, they're running a sale. Wanted to make sure I didn't miss out." I seriously had to work on my lying.

"Sissy's terrific."

Ah, there's my window! "Actually, I was talking with a woman named Ronnie."

"Yes, Ronnie Jones. I know her well."

Well enough to know she may have committed a murder? "Is that so?"

"Ronnie lives a few blocks north. She's not enamored with her new neighbors. We often get a call from her telling us their music is too loud. Apparently, the son who lives there is a deejay. Ronnie doesn't have a very high tolerance for noise or for people not following the rules or, well, anything." He chuckled.

Ronnie was intolerant? Interesting. "She was telling me she was a writer."

"Oh, I didn't know that."

"Yeah, she said she knew Marlena Ryder. Ronnie said she was at the bookstore yesterday, too."

"Yes, I know," he said. "Practically half of Salem was there. Marlena Ryder is very popular around here. I mean, *was*."

"How is the investigation going?" I asked, and Callahan's body language changed. He crossed his buff arms across his chest.

"You'd have to ask homicide detective Greg Daniels. He's investigating."

"Oh, I thought *you* were ... you know. Since you were at the bookstore."

"Daniels arrived after you left. He was out of town on vacation, but came back early. Homicide's his bag. At least for now."

Something told me Callahan wanted homicide to be *his* bag, too.

"Well, I'd better go," I said. "I've got the plumber coming today."

"Fixing up the old Kensington place, huh?" Callahan said.

"Yeah, hoping to turn it into a bed-and-breakfast."

"Great idea. That place could use some good publicity. Enjoy your day, Mrs. Kelly," he said and walked off.

I watched him go. What did he mean by that? Did he know something about the house's history? About William?

As I began walking home, my phone pinged. A text from Sebastian:

Hi. I had a last-minute grooming cancellation Sat morning at 11 a.m. Does that work for you and Boy?

If only a hairy Shih Tzu was the worst of my problems. I made a mental note to get back to Sebastian after my visit with the plumber as I hurried back home.

Chapter 8

"Thank you for coming. I'll see you soon," I said to the plumber, closing the door behind him.

"May I enter?" William asked from somewhere in the room.

"Sure."

William appeared in the entryway from the living room. I was happy to see him. I couldn't stop thinking about what Officer Callahan had said, about how this house could use some good publicity. It was easy to discount Mavis down at the historical society and think she had been wrong about William being a traitor, but when another Salem resident said something similar about Kensington House, it was hard to discard it again.

"Did all proceed smoothly with the plumber person?" William asked.

"Yeah, it's not as bad as I thought. I mean, it's still going to be expensive to get this place up to date. Looks like I'm going to have to install a new water heater. You don't have any idea the last time pipes were replaced in this building, do you?"

William thought about it and shook his head. I imagined the years passed by in a blur when you were haunting a house. Especially if there were no residents. Nothing and no one to keep you occupied.

"Water heater?" he asked, his brow furrowed.

"Yeah. C'mon, I'll show you."

I grabbed a flashlight and walked toward the basement door.

Bark!

"Boy, you stay here. I'll be right back."

I slowly crept down the stairs. I had never really been to this part of the house until the plumber arrived. He seemed to know the way to the basement since a lot of the homes, he said, had the same layout. I didn't even realize the basement door was there, tucked into the left side of the kitchen.

When I reached the bottom, William appeared in front of me. Apparently, he didn't want to deal with the rickety old steps. I wouldn't either if I didn't have to. I shined my flashlight around. As spooky as it was down here, the basement was dry, and there didn't seem to be any mold or rodent infestation. I might be shelling out tens of thousands of dollars for an electrician and a plumber, but at least I didn't have to call an exterminator.

"The plumber said this house has good bones," I said to William. For some reason, the statement made me proud as if he had complimented my child. I went toward the room the plumber had led me to, which had a bunch of pipes all leading to a large metal canister that was rusted and old.

"This old thing," I said to William somewhere in the dark. I couldn't see him, but I knew he was there. I could *feel* him. "The plumber thinks it was probably installed sometime in the 1950s or '60s. He's not sure, though. He'll have to replace a lot—if not most—of the pipes, he figures, too. He won't know until he 'opens things up,' as he said." The thought of putting holes in the walls gave me anxiety, but I guess you needed to break a few eggs to make an omelet. "I hope you don't mind. It's going to be noisy around here for a while."

"I'll be fine."

I didn't expect William to fuss. He never did. About anything. So kind and easygoing. Unlike the demanding ghost who was waiting for me to solve her murder. I shined the flashlight around at the rest of the basement and started to walk around carefully, making sure I didn't step on any loose nails. "Do you come down here much?" I asked.

"No," he said. "Not any longer."

The basement was segmented into a main room that fed off into a few smaller rooms, and then a tiny, closet-sized space with an old toilet. A water closet. "Were these bedrooms?" I asked, pointing to the smaller rooms.

"For a time."

I couldn't imagine who would want to sleep down here. There were no windows that I could see. I walked across the main room until I reached some exposed plumbing. If my calculations were correct, I was standing underneath the bookshelves in the living room. On the wall was a large piece of wood covering what looked like a doorway. "Where does this lead?"

"Upstairs," William said.

"Upstairs where?" I couldn't remember seeing any doorways and then I remembered. "The secret rooms?"

He nodded. "This stairwell reaches the upper stairwell that serves the back of the house."

"And also goes outside, right?" I remembered standing in those rooms and feeling the breeze. I hadn't been back there since the day I found Joe standing in the bedroom.

"That is correct."

I shined my flashlight on William's ashen face. "What were these rooms used for?"

He hesitated. "Many things."

A noise from upstairs. It sounded like Ghost Cat was knocking things off the dining table again.

"I will investigate the clatter," William said, "and leave you to your exploring."

"Wait, William, you don't have to go!" I said, but it was too late. He had vanished. Too bad. I felt like William was finally going to tell me something about this old house.

Mavis and Officer Callahan entered my brain. Did these rooms have to do with the bad history of this house and with William supposedly being a traitor?

I kept walking, shining my flashlight on the walls. In the corner, where the fireplace would be upstairs, was some writing. I couldn't make it out. Looked like numbers.

4533009

I shined my light on it and took a photo with my camera. Then in another corner were some letters.

AXJLEKTN

I snapped another photo. What did it mean?

A knock on the front door upstairs startled me. Who could that could be? Wiggins, maybe? I didn't have any more appointments scheduled for the day.

I began walking toward the staircase when I shined my flashlight on the floor near the boarded-up door to the secret rooms. There was a square piece of furniture, like an ottoman, made of wood. I wondered if it was made by a local artisan back in the seventeen or eighteen hundreds. Maybe I could bring it upstairs and have an interesting furniture piece in the living room. Something guests could admire. I pulled it away from the wall and shined my flashlight on the back, but I was distracted by what was *under* the piece of furniture.

A raised square of wood. I bent down and ran my hands along it, praying I didn't get a splinter. It moved a tiny bit when I pushed on it. I put the flashlight between my knees and placed both hands on the side of the wood and pulled up. It gave, and I fell backward onto the basement floor, with the piece of wood still in my hands.

What the …?

Knock, knock.

Bark!

"I know, Boy! I hear it! I'm coming!" He must have been standing at the top of the stairs.

I picked up the flashlight and shined it into what looked like a two-by-two-foot hole in the floor.

"What is this?" I said aloud. A trapdoor? Hidden in the basement floor? Where did it lead?

Knock, knock.

Bark!

"I'm coming! I'm coming!" I called as I hurried up the staircase, wondering why there was a trapdoor in the basement. And some weird numbers. And letters. And whether it had anything to do with the curious history of Kensington House.

Chapter 9

I OPENED THE FRONT door, and Marlena was standing there, the sun flittering through her translucent gray body. "Took you long enough," she said.

"Sorry. I was in the basement."

She stood there as if waiting for something. "Well?"

"Well, what?"

"Aren't you impressed?"

"Impressed with what?"

"Seriously?" She crossed her arms, apparently upset that whatever it was wasn't obvious to me. "I figured out how to knock on a door." She threw out her hands in a ta-da way.

"Oh, um, that's great." I knew my enthusiasm seemed lackluster, but I couldn't stop thinking about the trapdoor in the basement.

"I also learned how to sit on a bench." She looked for a reaction from me and, when she didn't get one, rolled her eyes. "I know it's not as exciting as when you dog people teach your mutts to poop on command, but this was a big deal for me. It really isn't that difficult once you get the hang of it. Just have to have the right frame of mind. Like not thinking about it and yet thinking about it at the same time."

I had no idea what that meant but was happy it worked for her. "Where were you? I thought we were supposed to meet at Haute Chocolate."

"Well, I hurried to Haute Chocolate once I got out of the library, but you must have been already gone. Any developments?"

"No, not really. Just that the woman Ronnie is trying to get published."

"The more I think about it, the more I think she might have had something to do with it. As you said, jealousy can cause us to do awful things." She made the motion of pulling air into her lungs in a deep inhale. "You just never know when—" She stopped talking and looked past me, inside the house. "I thought you said no ghosts were allowed in your home."

I turned around. William was standing behind me. "No visiting ghosts. William lives here."

"He *lives* here?" She sized William up. "So, what's your story?" she asked him. "Somebody murder you, too?"

I stayed quiet, wondering what William would say. He just stood there, looking at her curiously. "Unfinished business, I suppose," he said finally.

"I'm assuming you weren't murdered at your own book signing," she said with another fake but long sigh. "An event that was supposed to be one of the *happiest* of my career." Marlena appeared to be turning up the drama. Like she had at the book signing. *Stage* Marlena. She reminded me of someone I used to work with at my first job after college.

Ghost Cat hopped out of the house and into the driveway, and Marlena took a step back. "What is this place?" she asked. "The land of the lost?"

"There's not much more I can tell you, Marlena," I said, trying to get our discussion back on track. "I didn't really get that much time to talk with this Ronnie person."

"Why not?"

I was too embarrassed to tell her I got freaked out being alone with her. Before I could say anything, though, she said, "Never mind. Tonight's Thursday night. The writers' workshops take place on Thursday. I think we should go and see what's going on. Get a feel for things."

Ugh. I had my heart set on taking one of the books in the living room's vast library and curling up under a blanket, dusty or otherwise. "Where is it being held?"

"At the library."

The library?

My breath hitched. As much as investigating Marlena's murder didn't appeal to me, the thought of going to a library made my heart sing. "All right. What time does the meeting start?"

"Around seven p.m."

"I'll meet you there."

"Sounds good." She looked at William. "You can go, too, if you'd like."

"That is most kind, but I'll pass, thank you." He nodded. "Good day," he said and vanished.

"Man of few words," Marlena said.

Yeah. *Too* few sometimes, I had to admit.

"All right," she said. "I'll see you tonight. I'm going to spend the day practicing sitting on benches and knocking on doors."

"Sounds like fun." (Not.) I watched her go, imagining all the people who would be answering doors in downtown Salem, only to open them and find nobody there.

Chapter 10

THE SALEM PUBLIC LIBRARY was located on Essex Street, a few blocks from the Salem Historical Society. It was housed in a renovated brick mansion that, I read online, was originally owned by a sea merchant whose family donated the building to the city of Salem. I loved that I was going to live in a place that had a centuries-old respect for reading and the power of books. Seemed like my kind of town.

In the lobby was a bulletin board with people gathered around it, pointing at the various sheets of paper that had been posted there. One had a black-and-white photo of an animal with the words *Lost Dog* written in big, block letters above it. I froze. But the dog looked too big and tall to be Boy, and I didn't see any other postings about an adorable little black-and-white Shih Tzu.

Another notice on the bulletin board caught my eye.

Monthly Meeting
Salem Small Business Group
New Members Welcome

I took note of the meeting's date and time. I knew I had ghosts on my mind, but I really had to start thinking of myself as a businessperson and decided I would work up the nerve to go to an upcoming meeting of the Salem Small Business Group.

As I walked inside the main doors of the library, goosebumps shot up my arms. I couldn't remember the last time I had stepped foot in a library. Definitely before my marriage to Joe. I missed the smell of books. The sound of pages turning. The gazillions of stories waiting to be read. I felt myself being pulled toward the stacks.

But there was no time. I looked at my watch. I had about an hour before I had to meet Marlena for her writers' workshop. That should be plenty of time to find out if what I had been hearing about William and Kensington House was incorrect. Because that's what I hoped—that it was incorrect. That, instead of being a traitor, William was a do-gooder Union soldier who loved his mom and his wife and took in stray pets and fed the hungry. Actually, I'd settle for anything in between the two.

I walked into the main lobby and toward the reference desk. A young woman was on the phone. When she was done, she put a smile on her face and looked up at me. "Hi, can I help you?"

"Hi, I'm looking for information on Salem's history."

"Well, we have a lot, as you can imagine. Is there anything in particular you're looking for? Is this about the witch trials?"

"No, actually. I was more interested in the homes."

"Architecture?"

I thought of the trapdoor I had found. "Well, not exactly."

The librarian looked confused.

"I moved into one of the historic homes in the neighborhood, and I'm interested in learning more about it."

"Oh, how exciting. Which home is it?"

How had Mavis referred to it? "I think it's called Kensington House."

The librarian's smile disappeared.

"What's the matter?" I asked.

"Nothing," she said in a way that made me not believe her. "Well, I don't think you'll have any trouble finding information on *that* home." She punched a few letters on her keyboard. "Did you try the historical society?"

"Yes, but I didn't get very far." That was one way of putting it.

"Well, they have all kinds of information. Scans from deeds. Maps of property lines. You can also visit the offices of the *Salem Chronicle*, which recently digitized all their back issues. Their archives go back to the early eighteen hundreds, I believe. There would be lots of stories about the residents of that home there."

"Really? What kind of stories?"

She didn't answer as she typed a little more, making me feel like I had just moved into Salem's version of Long Island's Amityville Horror House. A nearby printer spit out a document. She picked it up and handed it to me. "These are some books that may get you started. Our history section is right there." She pointed to the back of the library.

"Great. I appreciate it."

As I walked toward the section she had indicated, I skimmed the list of book titles in my hand:

Villains of the Civil War

Notorious Figures in New England History

The next title made me stop walking.

Little-Known Traitors of American History

Traitors. There was that word again.

I hurried toward the history section and found the first book in the stacks. I sat on a cushioned bench and flipped to the book's index, scanning the page until I reached the words *William Kensington, p. 59.*

I didn't move. Part of me didn't want to look at page 59. But the other part of me knew I had to.

I flipped to the correct page and braced myself. At the top was a photo of William, and I couldn't help but smile. He looked the same as he did now but in a different type of gray. More of a sepia tone that was common for photos of the day. But he looked *human.* There was definition in his cheeks. His hair appeared to be dark, probably brown.

He still had those piercing eyes, which I knew to be pale blue. And there were those thick eyebrows he had a habit of furrowing. And the uniform he had a habit of straightening. The photo was a reminder that William Kensington had been a real person. Somebody's husband. Somebody's son. Somebody's comrade in arms.

My eyes wandered to a small paragraph of text under the photo, and my smile disappeared.

William Kensington (1825 – 1863)

William Kensington was born on June 7, 1825, in Salem, Massachusetts. He was married on January 27, 1855, to Mary Ann McCall of Salem, Massachusetts. Following her decease, he married Flora McKinsey in February 1861.

William had been married twice?

Kensington served in the Union army during the Civil War, enlisting in 1861 in the 55th regiment mustered in at Camp Meigs in Readville, Massachusetts, near Boston. He was convicted of treason and of the murder of Nathan Newbury on October 3, 1863, and sentenced to death.

My heart began to pound.

He died on October 17, 1863, at the age of thirty-eight years, four months and ten days by hanging.

I sat back in my chair. It was worse than I had imagined. Not only had William been convicted of treason, but *murder*? And he had been *hanged*? Every film and television show I had ever watched that featured a hanging came to mind. I didn't want to believe it, but there it was. In a book that, I assumed, had been vetted and copyedited and then carefully cataloged and placed in this beautiful library. It had to be true.

I flipped through the rest of the book, but there was nothing more about William, other than a photo of him on the next page with John Wilkes Booth.

John Wilkes Booth! What??!!

No further details of this alleged treason. The rest of the book was devoted to more well-known soldiers associated with Confederate espionage. William was just a traitorous footnote in American history.

I flipped back to the page with William's headshot. *That* was the person (er, ghost) I knew. But the words surrounding that image didn't make sense. The facts collided violently with what I felt to be true about William. I had learned how to read people—find out who they were on the inside, which often had nothing to do with who they were on the outside—and my heart told me that this couldn't be true. With William, I sensed kindness. And empathy. And sadness rather than anger. There wasn't hate in his heart. I knew people with hate in their heart. Like Joe. And his sister,

Allison. And yet, there it was. On my lap. In black and white. And sepia.

It just couldn't be.

But why couldn't it?

William Kensington was human. And humans were flawed. William Kensington was no less flawed than the rest of us.

I didn't know how long I was sitting there, but a woman wearing a large gold pin in the shape of a book approached me to tell me the library would be closing in ten minutes. Already?

"I'm supposed to meet someone here at seven o'clock," I whispered. "For a writers' meeting."

"The meetings are held in the downstairs rooms, which are open until nine p.m.," she explained. "But if you'd like to check out a book," she glanced at the book in my lap, "please do so now."

As she walked toward the exit, people were hurrying toward the front desk with piles of books in their hands. I looked at the two other books on the list the librarian had given me. Would those books say the same as this one? That William was a traitor? A black mark in American history? *Besties with John Wilkes Booth?*

I closed the book on my lap and was about to place it back on the shelves when I changed my mind. *Maybe I should take it home? Confront William?*

Confront was the wrong word. It connoted guilt. Maybe *ask* him about it?

I carried that no-good, lying textbook to the front desk. When it was my turn in line, I said, "I'd like to check out this book, please." I really wanted to burn it. But I'd settle for taking it home.

"I'll need your library card," the librarian said. He had a friendly smile that softened the creases of his wrinkled forehead.

"I don't have one yet. I just moved to Salem."

"Well, I'll need some ID with your current address, and I can make one for you now."

"Um, I don't have that either."

The friendly smile turned dubious. "Well, then I'm afraid I can't let you check out that book until you can provide confirmation of address. I'm sorry."

I stepped out of the line and walked back to where I had found *Villains of the Civil War*. I took out my phone and snapped photos of the two images featuring William and the accompanying text. That would have to do for now. Then I hurried out of the library where a ghost who had also been put to death was waiting for me.

Chapter 11

Marlena was standing by the stairwell. *Leaning* on the handrail, actually. All that practice with touching things had been paying off. If she hadn't been completely gray and translucent, she could have passed for a regular person just hanging out by the library's entrance. I took out my phone and placed it by my ear.

"Were you in the *library*?" she asked. As if that was the last place I'd ever be.

"I'll have you know, I practically *lived* in my local library all through school. Including college. It was my second favorite place, outside of home."

She looked at me like I was weird. Which *I* thought was weird. Wouldn't an *author* like being in a library?

"The writers' workshop takes place downstairs," she said.

"Yeah, I know. One of the librarians told me."

She looked at me closely. "Are you all right?"

No, I wasn't all right. Far from it. I had just found out that my only friend in the world was hated by the entire country. That Civil War historians probably had William's sepia-toned face on a dartboard in their stuffy offices. But I just nodded. "I'm fine."

"Okay, good. Let's go."

We followed a crowd of people heading to the lower level. Apparently, the writers' workshop wasn't the only thing going on after hours. There was a seminar on financial planning in one room and a salsa dancing class in another. On the right, a few women were milling around a big posterboard sign on an easel that had a photo of Marlena and the words *Rest in Peace* below it.

Marlena lingered among them for a bit, enjoying their grief and their gushing about her writing, but then her face changed. "Game on," she said as we walked into the room.

I took a deep breath and tried to get William out of my head. I needed to focus. I could only deal with one ghost at a time.

The room was filled with about a dozen people. All of them writers. Somehow, they *looked* like writers. It wasn't their clothing that gave them away—there wasn't one blazer with patches on the elbows among them. Just an academic look. I tried to blend in like I was one of them. Impostor syndrome wasn't new to me. I experienced it every time I was out socially with Joe's friends and pretended to be an adoring wife.

I stepped toward a table covered with donuts and cupcakes. I recognized the Flutternutter from The Haunted Cookie immediately. I reached for one.

"Those aren't for you," Marlena scolded, trying to slap my hand, although her fingers went right through it. Apparently, she needed more practice. "They're for the *writers*."

Embarrassed, I pulled back my hand. Chastised by a ghost? Really?

"There." She pointed. "Take a seat near the back. That's where the newbies usually sit while the established writers sit at the conference table."

She said the words *established writers* with condescension. Like I was back in high school and trying to join the school newspaper.

I took a seat next to an older woman with brown, brassy-ish hair, probably in her sixties, who was clutching a looseleaf binder in her hands. "Hi," she said.

"Hi," I said back. She looked more nervous and out of place than I did.

"Funny seeing you here!" Ronnie Jones plopped down on the other side of me.

"Well, well, well," Marlena said, standing over Ronnie with her arms folded. "Look who's here. My murderer."

"You don't know that," I said.

"Don't know what?" Ronnie asked.

"Oh, I'm sorry. I was talking to myself. I do that some-times."

She laughed. "Well, you'll fit in just fine around here. Talking to yourself is an occupational hazard for writers." She laughed again. "But I thought you said you weren't a writer."

"I'm not. I mean, I wasn't, but talking to you got me thinking that maybe I should start writing stuff down that I think about. No harm in trying, right?"

"Absolutely." Ronnie put her hand on my arm. "That's wonderful. If there's anything you need, just let me know." She got up and walked toward the conference table.

"Don't let her fool you," Marlena whispered. "She's a barracuda. An editing barracuda."

"Why are you whispering?" I asked. Nobody seemed to notice her. The woman next to me was busy flipping through the pages of her binder, which was filled with all kinds of red pen marks. If I hadn't known better, I would have thought she had bled on the pages of her book. I knew writing was hard, but could it be *that* hard?

Once Ronnie sat down at the conference table, another woman I recognized from Marlena's book signing stood up. I couldn't remember her name.

"Welcome, everyone. I'm so glad to see lots of old and new faces here. Unfortunately, we are here under very sad cir-cumstances. Marlena Ryder had been a longtime member of this writers' group. Many of us knew her well. And also knew her *when*. I thought we could begin tonight's workshop with a short reading from Marlena's best-selling book."

As the woman began to read, Marlena sat down next to me in the chair Ronnie had vacated and leaned back. She was definitely getting more comfortable in her ghostly body.

I covered my mouth and whispered, "Who's that woman talking?"

"That's Margaret Sherwood. She's been running the writers' workshop for years. She writes poetry. Not my cup of tea. But very good."

I nodded, wondering if Salem's poet laureate would have any reason to slice Marlena Ryder's throat.

"I stared into his eyes and wondered if he was the kind of man who would do me harm," Margaret Sherwood read. "The kind of man my momma told me to watch out for. As he painted the walls of my bedroom teal, covering the little-girl pink, he glanced at the photos of me and my friends, and I was embarrassed. I wanted him to look at me as a woman. Not a little girl. Yes, I was only sixteen, and he was in his twenties, but I felt drawn to his eyes. The power of his gaze. And the strength of his hands as I watched the bristles of the paintbrush bend this way and that. Little did I know those hands would squeeze the life from me in less than twenty-four hours." Margaret paused. "Marlena did love her thrillers, didn't she?" she asked the room.

Heads bobbed up and down.

"Sales of *The Secrets We Keep* skyrocketed after Marlena's death," Margaret added. "They're saying the book is now one of the fastest-selling books of all time." She cleared her throat, getting a little verklempt. "Is it all right if we take a few minutes?"

"Of course," Ronnie said. "Everyone, look over the work that you're sharing today. We'll be right back."

As some of the writers at the conference table got up, I said, "I'm having a donut."

"But," Marlena protested, "they're not—"

I left her there and walked to the snack table, reaching for a Fluffernutter.

"Those are my favorite," Ronnie said, reaching for one as well.

Just then, Alice from The Haunted Cookie walked in.

"Hi, Alice!" Ronnie said. "Great donuts!" Alice gave a small smile and took a seat in the back.

"Alice is a writer?" I asked.

"I think so," Ronnie said. "She comes to a lot of meetings. She doesn't say much. She sits in the back. She's very shy. I wish I could say the same for most of the writers here."

"What do you mean?"

"Unfortunately, most writers think a lot of themselves. They come here and they read their chapters or their scenes, and they're not really looking for any criticism. They just want to be told how great they are."

"Maybe they're just looking for a bit of encouragement."

She took a bite of her donut. "They're feeding their own egos. Trust me, I try to help. I try to offer tips on grammar and punctuation, but most writers aren't interested. There are software programs that can do that stuff for them now. No need to learn." She exhaled loudly. "Far be it from me to speak ill of the dead, but Marlena was kind of like that."

I glanced at Marlena, who was standing near the conference table, reading some of the pages lying about.

"You didn't think she was very good?" I asked.

"No, she *wasn't* very good. It wasn't an opinion. It was a fact," Ronnie said. "I would offer her tips week to week, and she ignored them. She just wanted the fortune and fame."

I looked into Ronnie's eyes. Was that jealousy I saw? "Well, *somebody* must have thought it was good. Good enough to publish."

"My first thought—when Marlena was parading around, talking about signing with a literary agent—was that good taste is subjective. And people will publish anything nowadays if you have enough social media followers. But ..." She took another bite of her donut. "Then I read her book. *The Secrets We Keep*. I have to say, it was *good*."

"Really?"

She nodded. "Surprised the heck out of me. I realized that Marlena had listened to a lot of my advice here. Meanwhile, all along, I thought she hadn't been listening at all. She would usually roll her eyes or tell me I was jealous. But *The Secrets We Keep* is a solid thriller. Suspenseful. A page-turner.

It deserves every accolade it got. Every success. I wish I had been able to tell her that. I had been planning to tell her at the book signing. And never got the chance."

"All right, everyone!"

Margaret was back. She must have gotten a drink or something because her coloring was better.

"Well, back to critiquing!" Ronnie said. "Again, if you have any questions or want to talk privately—it can be a little overwhelming to share here—feel free to stop by Haute Chocolate any time. I'm there Tuesdays and Thursdays."

"Thanks," I said as she returned to the conference table. "I will."

I sat back down in my seat with half a donut in my hand.

"This is my first time here," said the sixty-something woman to my right.

"Mine too. I'm Clara."

"I'm Martha. My husband thinks I'm crazy to start writing at my age." She smiled sheepishly.

"Not crazy at all. You never know when the desire will hit you to try something new. I just decided this year to open a bed-and-breakfast."

"How wonderful!" She motioned to the others in the room. "I just don't know if I'm ready. Everyone here looks so accomplished."

"I don't think they are. I think they just look that way. Fake it till you make it, right?"

"I don't know. Maybe my husband was right. I think I'm going to go." She picked up her purse from the floor.

It pained me to see a wife let her husband influence what she could and couldn't do. I knew quite a bit about that. But I understood that people did things in their own time. And I prayed Martha would. "Maybe I'll see you here again one day."

"Maybe," she said and hurried out the door.

"I thought she'd *never* leave," Marlena said, watching Martha go and sitting in her vacated chair.

"It takes a lot of guts to come here and, you know, share," I whispered, covering my mouth.

"You clearly have never been to one of these workshops before. People share way too much. Anyway ..." She waved her pale gray hand in the air dismissively. "What did good ol' Ronnie have to say? Anything about me? About murdering me in the local bookshop?"

"I don't think she did it."

"And you know that because ..."

"Just a sense."

"A sense, huh?" Marlena shrugged. "Well, forgive me if that's not quite good enough. I think we'll have to do some more sleuthing."

"You know," I stood up, "I changed my mind. I don't like your tone. I don't like the way you talk to or about people. I get you're a best-selling author. And that's pretty awesome. But it doesn't give you a license to be a jerk."

With that, I walked out the back door of the conference room just as I heard Margaret Sherwood ask, "Who wants to share first?"

Chapter 12

For the first time I could remember, I walked into Kensington House hoping I *wouldn't* see William. I didn't know how to discuss what I had learned about him at the library. I didn't want it to change our relationship but feared it would.

It was still light outside when I opened the door, and Boy came running toward me with my blond wig hanging from his mouth.

"Hi, sweetie. Let's get your leash and get to the hotel."

"May I enter?" William's voice emanated around the room.

"Of course," I said, even though I wasn't sure I wanted him to.

He appeared near the kitchen as if I had caught him fixing himself something to eat. I busied myself getting Boy's leash and harness.

"How fared your visit to the library?" he asked.

"Oh, it went okay." I was afraid to look at him. Afraid I'd see that sepia-toned expression on his face. That I'd imagine John Wilkes Booth standing right beside him.

"Does something preoccupy your thoughts?" he asked.

"No, not at all."

That was the first time I had lied to William. A piece of me died inside. I couldn't do this. William was my friend. I didn't want to start hiding things from him. I didn't want to live my life this way anymore. "Actually," I said. "That's not true. There *is* something on my mind."

"Very well. What is it?"

I looked at his face. The kindness in it. Was it possible for a face to be that kind and also be traitorous? I knew it was. I lived with that kind of man for years. But after time, I had learned to see through Joe's duplicity. William's kind face seemed genuine. But hadn't Joe's at first?

I was about to ask him. Just push the words out of my mouth when I saw something hanging on the wall.

"Does it please you?" William asked, following my gaze.

William's Ground Rules. The browned piece of paper I had framed. He had hung it on the wall right near the front door. Tears formed in the corners of my eyes.

William adjusted his jacket. "Would you prefer it relocated?" he asked.

"No, William. It's fine. It's perfect. Very thoughtful, thank you."

"Very well." He waited. "You did mention something weighing on your mind."

I glanced at the rules. Rule Number Four. *Don't ask about the past.* Hadn't I promised William to accept him as he was? Just as he had accepted me when I came storming into his life—well, into his *existence.* Shouldn't I do the same for him? But I didn't want to lie.

"I was thinking," I said, "that maybe we could amend my ground rules. Not *these.*" I pointed to the document hanging on the wall. "Mine."

"I'm afraid I don't understand."

"I mean, the rule where I asked you to announce yourself every time you walked into a room. I don't think we have to do that anymore."

"No?"

I shook my head. "I know when you're here. I don't know how. But I do. I can sense you. I couldn't when I first got here. But now I know you're here as if you are any other person. Just like I could tell when Joe was in the room after a while. He would try to sneak in sometimes and spy on me, but the air changes when a person—or a spirit—enters. Most people don't realize it. So, it would make me happy if you just walked around this beautiful old house the way you always have for more than a hundred years. You don't know how much it means to me that you would alter your ways just for me. To make me comfortable. But now you don't need to."

William nodded. "Very well. Thank you, Clara."

"No, thank *you*, William." And before he could ask me if there was *anything else* on my mind, I snapped Boy's leash onto his harness. "I'll be back tomorrow morning, William."

"Are you departing for the hotel?"

"Yes."

"Very well." He adjusted his jacket. "The house is silent in your absence. I had grown accustomed to the stillness—yearning for it for the years others dwelt here. Now, it feels almost too quiet at times." He didn't wait around for a response and disappeared.

I think William just told me he misses me when I'm gone. I smiled.

Bark!

"Yes, I know. He's pretty great, isn't he?"

I grabbed my purse, glancing at the framed document of William's Ground Rules on the wall—and, particularly, at Rule Number Four, scribbled in pencil. Could I live here knowing what I know and not get William's side of the story?

In the past few months, I had proven I was capable of a lot of things.

But, somehow, this seemed like it might be the hardest of all.

Chapter 13

I RUBBED THE SLEEP dust from my eyes as I walked toward Derby's Downtown Market. Why did I take photos of that darn library book? I stared at them most of the night. And when I finally *did* fall asleep, I had a dream that John Wilkes Booth and William were in Atlantic City playing blackjack and Ghost Cat was the dealer. I bolted upright in bed and scared Boy half to death. For eight years, I had had nightmares about Joe; this was a surprisingly new twist.

As the market's large windows approached—advertising tuna fish cans and pasta sauce this week—I walked right by. Yes, when I dropped off Boy at the house, I had told William I was going food shopping. And I would. But right now, I just wanted to clear my head. It was a beautiful sunny day in Salem, and the air would do me good. And also keep me out longer than necessary. Because the truth was, I was avoiding William. In addition to avoiding Marlena.

Hiding from *two* ghosts. Lucky me.

I walked and walked, and when my legs felt rubbery enough, I knew I needed to turn back. I couldn't stay out here forever.

I looked around. *Where was I?*

The street sign read *Carlton Street*, which sounded familiar. Wasn't that the name of the street Marlena mentioned at the book signing? The street she once lived on? In a "pretty blue house," she said, if I remembered correctly.

What kind of house gives rise to a best-selling author?

I was surprised she sold it. My guess was most folks didn't give up these historic homes too easily. They were so darn charming. But as pretty and blue as this house supposedly was, it must have paled in comparison to the big, bright lights of New York City. And a life of fame and fortune. Marlena thought her dreams were too big for Salem. How funny that my own dreams (nightmares?) had brought me right here.

Most of the houses on Carlton Street had that little plaque on the front exterior, just like Mr. Wiggins's. So much history here. I'm sure there was a fascinating story for every house on the block. I thought of William. Every cell in my body told me he was no traitor. There had to be more to the story.

Carlton Street didn't appear to be that long, so odds were good that I would find Marlena's house quickly. Sure enough, the house was just a few doors down. It was the only blue house on the block. A charming place with a gravel driveway and white window boxes with peonies poking out their lovely pink heads. I imagined a younger Marlena somewhere inside, gazing out one of those windows, looking for inspiration. I had always marveled at how writers could create worlds inside their heads while sitting in an empty room, although I knew a little something about that living with Joe.

In front of the blue house, at the bottom of a short set of white wooden steps, was a small memorial. Wreaths, books, candles, and signs that read *Rest in Peace, Marlena*. This *was* the right house, after all. Tiny notes of condolences for the local writer turned best-selling author. Some flames just didn't get to burn long at all.

I walked to the side of the house and peered into the backyard. There was a green lawn near a firepit surrounded by light-blue-and-white striped patio furniture. No toys or bicycles to indicate that young children lived there. I wondered who bought the house.

I didn't have to wonder long because the front door of the home opened, and a woman stuck out her head. "Hello there! May I help you?"

Ugh. I felt like a stalker. The last thing I ever wanted to be. "Hi, no, so sorry to bother you. I was just walking by."

The woman stepped outside. She was wearing pink pastel pants and a loose-fitting white top, and her gray hair was short and neatly combed. "It's been so busy around here the past few days. Just quieting down now. Lots of folks upset with what happened." The woman walked toward me, stopping to adjust a memorial sign that had fallen over. "Did you know her? The author, Marlena Ryder?"

How to answer that? "Yes. I did." Actually, *do.*

"I only met her once. When I came to buy this beautiful home. My husband passed away a few years ago, and I wanted to make a change. Moved here from Ohio. Just wasn't the same in our home anymore without him there. Too many memories."

I could definitely relate. Although, I was sure, my memories of Joe were far less heart-warming than those of this woman's husband.

"Name's Anna, by the way. My son, Keith—he's a lawyer in Peabody—was looking for a place near here to use when he didn't want to commute into Boston. He told me I could move here. See more of my grandchildren. I couldn't say no."

"That sounds lovely. My name's Clara."

"Have you lived here long, Clara?"

"Just moved in a few months ago."

"Ah, so you're a newbie like me." She smiled. "Well, Clara, do you want to come inside? I'll show you around. I don't mean to be so forward, but I don't have very many friends around here and could use the company. Have you been here before? When Marlena Ryder lived here?"

"No. We met after she ... hit it big."

"Well, come on in. I'll make some tea."

There really was no reason for me to go inside, but my curiosity was getting the better of me. I wanted to see where Marlena Ryder grew up. I wanted to see what kind of house this was. Was there something thriller-y about it? Like ghosts? Trapdoors? No, wait, that was *my* house. "That's very kind of you. If you don't mind. I'll only stay a minute."

"Oh, don't be silly. Stay as long as you like."

As I followed Anna toward her dark blue front door, a thought occurred to me: What if this nice sixty-something woman had murdered Marlena Ryder? I wasn't sure if she had a motive, unless she felt she overpaid for her house. But she seemed nice enough. Something told me she was a good person—and I was learning to rely on that instinct more and more—so I went inside.

The entrance led into a cozy living room with walnut furniture and a maroon couch with sumptuous pillows. The early afternoon light was shining through the window, bouncing off the hardwood flooring, bringing warmth.

"You have a lovely home," I said.

"Oh, thank you."

A large room was adjacent to the living room, but instead of a big dining table, there was a small square table with four chairs.

"I like open space," Anna said. "No room for clutter in my life ever since my husband passed away. He was a pack rat." She laughed. "Sometimes I miss him yelling at me for throwing out the day's paper in the evening. 'The day hasn't ended yet, for Pete's sake, Ann!' He called me Ann." She smiled mournfully.

"It sounds like you had a wonderful marriage."

"Are you married?" She glanced at my ring finger.

"Widowed," I said. The word felt strange on my tongue.

"You as well? I'm so sorry." Anna patted my hand.

"Well, let's just say my marriage wasn't as wonderful as yours."

"Understood," Anna said with a nod. "Nothing more to say there then. Feel free to look around. Upstairs, take a look at the spare room on the right when you get to the top of the stairs. That, I believe, was Marlena Ryder's office."

"Are you sure you don't mind?"

"Not at all. Is Lipton tea all right?"

"That's just fine."

"And what a lovely necklace you have!"

I reached for my compass pendant and rubbed it. "Thank you. My dad gave it to me."

As Anna moved about the kitchen, I walked upstairs. A narrow hallway led to two rooms. The first looked like Anna's bedroom. A frilly blanket was on the bed, reminding me of the twin bed on the upstairs landing of Kensington House. Across from that, on the right, was what must have been the spare room. There was a desk with a computer, but not much else.

I walked into the room. Out the window was a charming view of the backyard, including the firepit and patio furniture. It was very possible that Marlena had penned her best-selling novel right here in this room. How exciting! There were footsteps behind me.

"The lighting is delightful in here, isn't it?" Anna said, stepping toward the window.

"It certainly is. It just bounces off the strip flooring."

"Oh, yes. My son had the floors refinished throughout the house. That reminds me. When the flooring in this room was refinished, the contractor found something." She pointed to a spot on the floor near the window. "One of the floorboards had been loose, and there were some things under there."

"What kind of things?"

"Odds and ends, it seemed. A bunch of letters wrapped with a rubber band. I'm ashamed to say I read some of them. Marlena Ryder seemed to be having some sort of affair with a married man long ago." Anna blushed.

"Really?" I wasn't sure if I was surprised.

"And also a looseleaf binder with lots of papers in it," she said. "It looked like a draft of someone's book. I began reading that too, but it was too scary for me. I don't read those kinds of books." She chuckled. "I love my romances and historical fiction."

I thought of Ronnie. "I met a woman in Salem who writes historical fiction. She's trying to get published."

"I imagine it's very hard nowadays." Anna went to a closet in the room and reached up onto a shelf. She pulled down a large manila envelope. "This is what was found under the floorboard. I called Marlena once or twice about it, but she never returned my calls. Maybe I had the wrong number. Or maybe she thought I had complaints about this house." She chuckled again. "And then, well, I just forgot about them—until this week. With the news of the murder. My son said I should sell these things on eBay now that Marlena's gone. He said they're probably worth a lot of money, but I'm not a *buttinsky*, as my grandma would say. It was Marlena's business." She opened the envelope and pulled out a wad of envelopes and a looseleaf binder filled with papers. The front cover of the binder read *Woman on the Run* by Penelope Givens.

"Is that the scary book?"

"Yeah, I never heard of it. Have you?"

"No. It looks like some kind of early draft." I took out my phone and searched for the title on Amazon, but nothing came up. "Marlena mentioned at the book signing that she worked with some authors. Maybe it was a book she was editing, or she was coaching the author. I'll ask her."

"I'm sorry?"

"I mean ..." *Nice going.* "I'll ask around. To see if maybe one of her writing workshop friends knows anything about it."

"I have to be honest," Anna said. "I had never heard of Marlena Ryder. I think I may have insulted her when I didn't know who she was. Do you think that's why she didn't take my calls?"

I shrugged, although knowing Marlena, that was very possible.

"Why don't you take this stuff?" Anna put the items back into the envelope and handed it to me. "You knew Marlena. You might know what to do with it."

"Oh, I'm not sure I—"

"You can bring it to that writers' meeting. Maybe they know this Penelope Givens person."

I took the package from her hands. "Okay. I'll ask around and see. Thank you."

A tea kettle whistled.

"Well, they're playing our song," Anna said.

I followed her downstairs, where she ushered me to the small dining table and brought out an antique tea set with a floral design.

"This is so nice, thank you." I placed the package on the chair next to me.

She sat down and poured the tea. "I should be thanking *you*. I'm always looking for ways to pass the time when my grandsons can't be here. I'm a retired teacher, K through 8, and work as a tour guide part time in downtown Salem. Boy, does it get busy here in the fall!"

"That's what I've heard."

"You can't even walk down Essex Street. They say sometimes there may be as many as a million people there. That's New York City on New Year's Eve crowds."

I couldn't imagine that cobblestone street being full of so many people.

"I was thinking of starting a book club," Anna said. "You know, as a way to meet people. Seems so hard nowadays to make friends as adults, don't you think?"

"I do." Little did Anna know that my only friend was a friendly neighborhood ghost. I took a sip of tea. "I'd love to join your book club. I've recently gotten into reading more." *That was one way of explaining it.*

"Really?" Her eyes brightened. "Well, that makes two people in the club, then. That's a good enough place to start. What kinds of books do you like to read?"

"All kinds," I said. "I'm open to anything." I thought of the shelves and shelves of books in my new home. "Once I get the electricity turned on in my house, we can have the meeting there."

"I would like that," Anna said, already refilling my teacup. I smiled.

I was making my first non-spectral, non-Shih-Tzu friend.

And for a girl who felt so alone for so many years, I couldn't have been happier.

Chapter 14

"EMILY, WHERE IS MY blue shirt? I told you I needed it for today."

Panic. Running through me like a current. I sat up on my side of the bed as night began to turn to morning. Did he tell me he needed his blue shirt today? I knew he didn't. I knew because he did this to me all the time. Blamed me for stuff he forgot. But what did it matter?

Joe came to my side of the bedroom, half dressed. His chest was wet from the shower, a sheen covering his muscled arms. How could I have ever wanted to be hugged by those arms? How could I have not known what they were capable of?

He grabbed my arm and yanked me off the bed. "Where is it?" he asked, his nostrils flaring. Like smoke was about to come shooting out of them.

"But," I said, "you didn't—"

"I didn't?"

I knew what was coming. I hadn't blamed myself. Like I was supposed to. Like a good little soldier. Or slave. And for that, I had to be punished.

A gleam appeared in Joe's eye. Then he lifted his hand, smiled, and I braced myself as—

I opened my eyes and sat up in bed.

Bark!

Boy hurried next to me, like he always did, settling next to my side, his little black-and-white butt scooching close to me. I breathed out slowly, trying to calm my racing pulse and remember where I was.

In a hotel in Salem.

Safe.

Joe was gone.

I was *safe.*

I lay back down, my head against the soft pillows. My rational mind understood all this. Why didn't my unconscious mind? I never figured on this when I was planning my escape. Never figured my husband would haunt me in my dreams. Even when I found a safe place. Even when I knew he couldn't hurt me anymore. Damn that Joe Turner. Wherever he was, he was certainly getting the last laugh.

I ran my hand over Boy's too-long coat.

Ugh. I forgot to text Sebastian back about the grooming appointment. Was it too late?

I grabbed my phone on the nightstand and texted him that I would take the 11 a.m. slot, if it was still available. It wasn't until I hit *Send* that I realized I was texting him at three o'clock in the morning. Great. In addition to being a weirdo who wore a crooked blond wig, he would think I was inconsiderate.

I tried to settle myself and think of good things. If I fell asleep too fast, Joe would still be there. Waiting for me. Like Freddy Krueger. I needed to get him off my mind and think of the good things in my life.

Like Boy. I rubbed his belly.

And William. Well, William who was considered a traitor, apparently.

So much for trying to think of good things. I was learning that good and bad were tied together more than I had thought.

What to do. What to do. Wait, I had a thought. On my phone, I navigated to the Salem Historical Society website and filled out the online application for the plaque for Kensington House. Yes, William's past was complicated and muddied, but I needed to move forward.

When I was done, my phone pinged. I looked at the screen. Sebastian was texting back? Already?

And here I thought I was the only one with insomnia. The slot is yours. See you tomorrow (today).

I hope I didn't wake him. Maybe he had bad dreams, too. I found my body beginning to relax as I stared at Sebastian's name. I put the phone down. I wasn't sure how to feel about that. Those green eyes were dreamy, but I wasn't ready to get into another relationship. I needed to find myself first. Learn from my mistakes. Men weren't the answer. That had been my first mistake. With Joe. Thinking I needed a man to get me where I wanted to go. Only *I* could take myself there. Once I was whole. And happy. And on my feet. Only then would I be ready for a relationship.

I scratched Boy's belly, and he lifted his paws to let me.

"Soon, we'll be sleeping in our own home with electricity and hot water," I told Boy.

I giggled. For a gal who had dreamed once of seeing the world, my aspirations really had changed. Now I dreamed only of a safe place and a sound sleep. Not with one eye open as I had done for years sleeping next to Joe.

I returned my phone to the nightstand and saw the manila envelope Anna had given me. I pulled it toward me, switched on the lamp, and sat up. *If I wasn't going to sleep, I might as well keep myself occupied.*

I pulled out the looseleaf binder. Why was this thing hidden under a floorboard? I could understand the forbidden love letters, but a book?

Why was she hiding it? And from whom? I gazed at the front cover.

Woman on the Run by Penelope Givens

I wondered if this was the only copy of the book. And whether it was any good. Apparently, it was too scary for

Anna to read. I opened to the first page, where there was a dedication:

For my mother, who has always been my biggest cheerleader. This book would not have been possible without your support.

My eyes watered. I imagined my own mother writing something like that to me. If she had been given the chance and not died of cancer when I was eight years old. I didn't remember much of her, only love—lots of love. And laughter. My father did his best so that I didn't feel the loss, but there was no getting away from the fact that my mother's death had left a hole in our lives. That was probably why my father never remarried. Never wanted to. Even after I told him I would be okay with it. "Once you've had the best, Emily," he said, "there's nowhere to go from there."

I shook away the memory. Why was I having so much trouble thinking of happy things? I gave Boy's belly another pat. My emotional support dog. I didn't know if pets had to take some sort of test to officially become one, but Boy would pass it with flying colors.

I turned to the next page of the manuscript and began to read:

Chapter One

Clare awoke with a start. Someone was watching her. She didn't know how she knew, but she knew. The air had changed. She sat up in bed, her eyes darting around the room. "Is some-

one there?" she asked. No answer. But then again, she didn't expect one ...

I stopped reading. Something about the passage sounded familiar. Like I had read it before. I kept going.

A noise. It came from downstairs. A clanking, like someone was fishing around for something. Clare reached under her bed for her pistol and checked to see if it was loaded.

I stopped again. I didn't remember that part. Only the beginning. Why did it sound so familiar?

I gasped.

Marlena. Wasn't this the passage she read at the book signing?

But how could that be?

I reached for my phone and searched on Amazon for Marlena's book, *The Secrets We Keep*. I clicked on *Read Sample*.

Melanie awoke with a start. Someone was watching her. She didn't know how she knew, but she knew. The air had changed. She sat up in bed, her eyes darting around the room. "Is someone there?" she asked. No answer. But then again, she didn't expect one.

I leaned back against the headboard. The passage was the same. The only thing different was the name. Melanie, instead of Clare.

Oh my God.

Had Marlena stolen someone's book? This Penelope Givens person? Is that why this manuscript was hidden under the floorboards in her office?

No, it couldn't be. That would be a brazen act. But wasn't Marlena a brazen person?

"Let's not get carried away. Right, Boy?"

Bark!

"There might be a perfectly logical explanation for this." Maybe Penelope Givens was Marlena's pen name. Or a name she used while she was writing earlier drafts. I had no idea how this author thing worked.

But then I remembered what Ronnie had said. That she hadn't liked any of Marlena's books. Until *The Secrets We Keep*. That Marlena hadn't had a handle on grammar or punctuation—until *The Secrets We Keep*.

A jolt of electricity shot through me.

Marlena Ryder had been keeping a *very* big secret.

Boy lifted his head and looked at me.

"Do you know what this means?" I asked him.

He licked my hand, which I took as a yes.

It meant that Marlena Ryder, the current belle of the publishing world, the number-one *New York Times* best-selling author, had stolen the book that was her claim to fame.

And it also meant something else.

That I had found my first serious murder suspect.

Penelope Givens.

My phone rang. I pulled it out of my pocket. I didn't recognize the number, but knew from the 978 area code that it was local. Unless it was spam. Ugh. I swiped anyway. "Hello?"

"Hello, Clara Kelly?"

"Yes, this is Clara."

"Hi, Clara. This is Greg Daniels. I'm a homicide detective with the Salem Police Department."

Goosebumps shot up my arms. I wasn't sure why. I hadn't done anything wrong. Did this have something to do with my being at Sadie's bookshop by the bathroom? "Hi, Detective," I said, trying to sound like it was every day that a police detective called my phone. "What can I do for you?"

"Would you be able to stop by down at the station?"

"When?"

"As soon as possible."

"Um, would I be able to stop by tomorrow afternoon?"

"That would be just fine. Thank you," he said, adding he would text the address.

I clicked off the call.

"A detective?" Marlena asked. "Is this about my case?"

"I think so. It was Greg Daniels. He wants to see me. I'll go tomorrow after we visit Boston Medical Center."

"Clara, listen. I can't go. Penelope might be in that terrible place because of what I ..." She paused as if unable to continue the sentence.

"Okay, fine. I'll go alone. I should be out of the house anyway. The electrician and plumber are starting work tomorrow, and I want to stay out of their way. A trip to Boston might just kill two birds with one stone."

Chapter 15

"Good morning!" Sebastian said.

He was standing at the counter when I walked into The Pampered Pup, looking ridiculously cute, with a wide smile that made his green eyes crinkle. He may have even gotten a haircut since the last time I saw him at Ye Olde Salem Book Shoppe.

I, on the other hand, looked a fright, I was sure. I hadn't slept a wink since reading the opening paragraph of Marlena Ryder's thriller novel. I told myself that maybe that opening paragraph was the only thing the same between Marlena's book and this Penelope Givens person's book, but after shelling out fifteen ninety-nine for the Kindle version of *The Secrets We Keep*, I discovered that wasn't true. Marlena's *entire book* was identical to this other book, practically word for word, with a few names changed here and there.

"Are you okay?" Sebastian looked at me as he bent down to pet Boy, who ran a few circles before lying on his back and exposing his belly.

"I'm fine," I said. "Just didn't sleep much last night." *Or the night before. Don't ask.*

"Yeah, I saw that. Insomnia?"

"I guess. Just have a lot on my mind."

"Well," Sebastian picked up Boy, who licked his cheek, "while Boy is getting pampered, maybe you should do the same. It's a beautiful day outside today. Go for a walk. Grab a quick bite. Let the sun shine on your face. I know that does wonders for me."

I appreciated the suggestions. But my plan was to spend that time finding Marlena and confronting her about my findings. "I'll see you in an hour and a half?"

"That's about right," he said. "But I'm here all day. Take as much time as you need. Boy won't be lonely. See you later."

Outside, I realized Sebastian was right. It *was* a beautiful day. I hadn't noticed on the walk from the hotel. I was always amazed at the things that could escape your attention unless you made a point to look for them.

I took a breath. Where would Marlena be? Well, where would a narcissistic, book-stealing author be at this time of day?

The Ye Old Salem Book Shoppe was crowded when I arrived. People were gathered at the front of the store around a memorial for Marlena. I recognized a few from the writers' workshop, including Margaret Sherwood, who was handing out flyers of some kind.

"Please join us for a vigil we're having in front of Old Town Hall at seven o'clock this evening," she said, handing a flyer to a woman holding a copy of *The Secrets We Keep*.

I glanced at Marlena's author photo on the back cover, and when I looked up, I saw her standing there, staring at me.

"I thought you were mad at me," she said. "You left the library in a huff."

I turned around and strode away from the bookshop, north toward Essex Street.

"Hey, wait a minute!" she called.

I kept walking until I reached a quiet corner with no one around. Then I stopped and let her catch up.

"What was that all about?" she asked when she got to me.

"What were you doing just now?" I asked.

"What do you think?" She crossed her arms. "Just hanging around. Listening to what people are saying about me and my book. I've practically given up on people seeing me. You're the only one, evidently. And now that I'm dead, I have few joys. At least it's nice to know that people like *The Secrets We Keep*."

"That's interesting."

"What's interesting?" Marlena asked.

"It's interesting that you referred to *The Secrets We Keep* as *your* book."

There it was. A tiny quiver of her right eyelid. Just a flicker. Like the fleeting glint I used to see in Joe's eyes when he was about to strike. A tell. I had learned to rely on them. Use them as a compass. A guide. Like the pendant around my neck my dad had given me.

Marlena furrowed her brow. "I don't know what you mean."

"Don't you?" I kept walking.

"Hey, where are you going? Are you really not going to tell me what this is all about?"

I came to a shaded bench right by a large tree and sat down. No one was around, but I took out my phone anyway and placed it to my ear. That Taylor Hampton was probably hovering somewhere, ready to catch me "talking to myself."

"I got to meet Anna," I said when Marlena caught up to me.

"You met who? Anna who?"

"The woman who moved into your home. A lovely lady."

"What does that have to do with anything?" Marlena said. "Wait, do you think she murdered me?"

"No." I rolled my eyes. "Of course not. But she did have some insights."

"Such as?"

"Well, she showed me this little hiding spot under the floorboards in one of the upstairs rooms."

I didn't have to go looking for tiny tells anymore because Marlena's face changed completely. Her smile disappeared, her cheeks fell, and her eyes gazed off into the middle distance. If I suspected moments before that she knew what I was talking about, now I was sure of it.

"Oh my God," she said, sitting on the bench next to me. "I completely forgot I had hidden it there."

"So, you admit it?"

Marlena looked at me. "You don't understand."

"I think I *do* understand."

"All my life, all I wanted to do was become an author. I dreamed of it when I was a little girl."

"That's no excuse for stealing."

"Penelope had attended a few writers' workshops a couple of years back. She usually just kept to herself. Stayed near the back. Where *we* sat the other day. One day, she approached me after the meeting and told me she was a thriller writer, too. She said she had written a manuscript and wanted to know what I thought about it. At the time, I was doing freelance editing to help pay the bills, and I told her if she left her manuscript with me, I would be happy to look at it and let her know what I thought—or give her an estimate of what my fees might be for a developmental or line edit."

"So, you're telling me she *trusted* you with her work?"

"Penelope was reluctant to leave it with me at first. She said it was the only copy she had. Had typed it on her grandfather's typewriter because she didn't have a computer. I told her that even if I couldn't work with her, at the very least I could input the manuscript for her so she'd have an electronic copy."

"How nice of you."

"I've worked with a lot of authors—some of them good, some of them okay, some of them with not really much talent. But once I started reading Penelope's book, I couldn't put the bloody thing down. It was great. Really great." She looked at me. "And I'll admit, I was *jealous*. I had been trying to find a literary agent for *years* with no luck."

"Like Ronnie. Only Ronnie didn't steal somebody's book."

"You make me sound so evil. It wasn't like that. Time went by, and I didn't hear from Penelope. I thought to myself, *Maybe this was meant to be. Maybe she wanted to give her book to someone to publish.*" I raised my eyebrows. "I don't know, you tell yourself all kinds of things when you're desperate. But I knew that taking that manuscript wasn't right. So, I decided to call Penelope and tell her how much I enjoyed her book and tell her my fee for inputting it for her. But when I called, her number was disconnected."

"How convenient."

"It really was. And then days, weeks, *months* went by, and I had this wonderful novel sitting in my house. I inputted the whole thing into a Word document, even though I didn't hear from her, and I loved it even more the second time. It had some nuance, things I hadn't noticed on the first read. And then ..."

"What?"

"I can't explain it, and you won't believe me, but over time, I began to think of the novel as mine." Marlena shrugged. "I started imagining what the characters looked like. I dreamed about them. Became obsessive about them. I changed a few names and made some plot changes here and there, and then I submitted it to a few agents, just to see what would happen." She looked at me with an innocent face. "And then I got a nibble. And then another. I was shocked. I had been pitching agents for *years* and barely ever gotten a response. Not even an email letting me know they received my manuscript. I knew I had something. And then—I don't know—it just became my book."

"It's not your book."

"Believe it or not, until you just said something, I had completely forgotten ..." She looked around as if someone might hear her confession.

"You forgot you *stole* it." I stood up. "I've heard enough."

"Listen, I'm not proud of my actions. What I did, I did out of desperation. And then, trust me, the stress got worse. The publisher was asking for a sequel. I'd been struggling with it."

I started walking.

"Where are you going?" she asked.

"That's none of your business. Whatever this is," I pointed to the two of us, "it's over."

"Please," Marlena said. "I'll do anything you want."

"Great. I want you to leave me alone."

Chapter 16

AFTER PICKING UP BOY and barely saying a word to Sebastian, I arrived home and unclipped Boy from his leash as if I was in a daze. On autopilot. I grabbed his food bowls, filled them, and placed them back down.

William appeared in front of me, and I was suddenly angry at him for not announcing himself even though I explicitly told him he didn't have to. "I don't know if you'll want to be in the same room with me," I said to him, tossing my keys on the dining table.

"What ails you?"

Oh, plenty ails me. "You want to know? Well, that ghost—Marlena Ryder, the one you met on the front steps—do you know what she did? She stole someone's book and published it as her own."

William's pale blue eyes widened. "That's falsehood."

"It's more than falsehood. It's intellectual property theft. I looked it up on my phone on the way home from the groomer." I could still see Marlena sitting up on stage at Ye Old Salem Book Shoppe with that confidence, gracing us all with her best-selling presence. How the audience adored her. How they fawned and gushed over her, not knowing what she really was. A thief. And a phony.

"This has troubled you," William said.

"Yes."

"For what reason?"

"For what reason?!" *How could he ask me "for what reason"? Wouldn't anyone be upset? Or was lying and IP theft small potatoes for a traitor?* "Is it really hard to understand why I'm upset?"

"Perhaps it's because you despise duplicity," he said calmly. "The idea of a person showing himself or herself as one way and really being another."

"Well, that's part of it, I guess. I lived with someone who was like that." *And possibly still am.*

"Perhaps." William looked down at the floor.

"You're not saying something. What is it you're not saying?"

"Well, I do not intend to distress you—but weren't you, too, duplicitous?"

"Me?"

"Yes," he said. "For years you conveyed the appearance of contentment to others. Those who were unaware of your circumstances."

"Yeah, but that's totally not the same thing."

He looked at me with that look. That *knowing* look.

"Okay, it *is* the same thing, but my reasons were different. I was scared of what Joe might do. Not really to me. He could slap me around all he wanted. It was my father. He threatened to hurt my father."

"Your duplicity stemmed from an insecurity. And I believe Miss Ryder's did as well."

I crossed my arms. "Are you saying I am no better than Marlena Ryder?"

"I'm suggesting that each of us carries our own burdens. We all cope in ways that may not be clear to others. All we can strive for is understanding, empathy, and growth from our errors."

I marched into the living room like an angry toddler. I sat on the couch and pulled a dusty blanket over me. Boy came running over, and Ghost Cat appeared, rubbing herself on one of the legs of the sofa. Boy tried to pounce on her, but she moved elegantly toward the coffee table and hopped on top.

William materialized in front of me. "I've upset you."

I sighed. "No, you haven't. It's just that … she wants me to help her. Marlena."

"Does she not deserve help?"

Okay, now I *was* getting upset. "Marlena committed a crime, William."

"And, might I say, she has received a far greater punishment than she deserves."

I stared at him. Were we still talking about Marlena? Or was William talking about himself?

"Please understand," William said. "There exists no justification for her actions. She may not even be penitent."

"She's not. I don't think she feels any guilt at all." Boy put his front paws on the side of the couch, and I pulled him onto my lap, where his newly groomed body settled upon my thighs. I fingered his black bowtie clip.

"Be that as it may, there are more constructive solutions to deal with what Miss Ryder did that do not involve violence."

I stared at him. Ugh, he was right. *Again.* "You make a valid point."

"I understand your rationale; however, individuals such as Marlena require our assistance and understanding. While you may disapprove of her actions, she did not deserve to perish for them. Violence has no rightful place in a civilized society." His gray face darkened, and he stared into my eyes. "I speak from experience."

Silence settled upon the room. I could hear Ghost Cat purring. And Boy's steady breathing. Was this my opening? Was William ready to talk about what had happened long ago? "William, what do you—" Before I could continue, my phone pinged in the dining room.

"Your rectangular magic communication device is summoning you," he said.

"It's not important."

My phone pinged again.

"I can wait." He pointed into the other room. "That cannot," he said and vanished.

"William!" I called, startling Boy.

I waited, but he didn't return. Ugh.

I gently placed Boy on the couch and hurried into the dining room, reaching for my phone. Two texts from Gus, the electrician. I texted him back and went into the living room, hoping William would reappear. He didn't. But Ghost Cat had made her way to the couch and was lying beside Boy, her tail lying on top of Boy's tail. They looked like crossed swords.

Great. My pets were happy, but I still didn't know what was going on with William. I sighed. He was right, though. Marlena may have been a thief, but she didn't deserve to be murdered. I put my phone back into my purse and wrapped the strap over my shoulder. I opened the front door.

Let me get this straight, I asked myself. *You're helping a thief and a plagiarist on the advice of a possible murderer and traitor to his country?*

Exactly, I answered myself. Then I stepped outside and went to find Marlena.

Chapter 17

Marlena wasn't hard to locate.

She was back at Sadie's bookshop, sitting outside. The people who had been standing in front of her memorial were gone, the candles melted down. When she saw me, her eyes darted away. "I thought you were done with me," she said when I stopped in front of her.

"Well, I thought I was, too."

"What changed?"

"Let's just say I got a little sense knocked into me."

I stiffened at my own words. Joe had said those words to me hundreds of times before. *I should knock some sense into you.* As a threat. I couldn't believe the sentence had just come out of my mouth. First, the nightmares. And now this? I figured it was going to take some time for my body and mind to rid themselves of Joe. As unaffected as I thought I was, his *being* somehow permeated my skin, crept into my psyche. Ugh. I couldn't wait to forget him altogether.

"By whom? That pale fellow you live with?"

I smiled. "Yes."

"He seems like a decent guy."

"He is. He said you didn't deserve what happened to you. And he was—" I stopped talking to let a family walk by. When they were out of earshot, I continued. "He was right. And—"

"So," Taylor Hampton said, striding out of Ye Olde Salem Book Shoppe. "I see you're still talking to yourself." He looked at my butt. "No phone in your pocket this time to use as an excuse."

This Hampton guy was pretty good at sneaking around. I should get him to do my sleuthing for me. "So, I like to talk to myself. It's not a crime."

Taylor took a seat on the bench right next to Marlena. He crossed his legs and his foot went through her knee. She scooted down a bit. I had the urge to walk away.

"I'm thinking I can crack the case," he said with assurance. "You know, the Marlena Ryder murder case."

"Why? What did you find?"

He smirked. "Like I would tell *you*."

"Well, I'm surprised you haven't interviewed me."

"Why would I interview *you*?" he asked, incredulous.

"I know Marlena pretty well."

"You mean *knew*." He laughed.

No, I mean, know. *Jerk.*

"They were able to identify just about everyone who was in the bookshop that day," he said.

"How?"

"The security footage from the streetlamps." He pointed at a camera that was positioned above the bookstore entrance. *Great, I'm sure the cameras had caught me talking to myself a bunch of times.* "And the photos Sadie had taken," Taylor said.

"Photos?" Marlena asked me.

That's right! Sadie had taken photos from the stage during the event. "You saw Sadie's photos?" I asked.

He laughed again. "*Everyone* can see Sadie's photos. They're on Instagram. You're not the greatest investigator. Luckily, that's not what you do for a living."

I glanced at Marlena. *See, I told you I wasn't good at this.*

"Hey!"

I looked up and saw Aaron, the guy who worked at the bookshop, coming toward me. "Local history, right?"

"Well, I'd better get going. I have leads to follow up." Taylor nodded at me and then at Aaron before strutting down the street.

"You know that guy?" I asked Aaron, watching Taylor go.

"Unfortunately. If it makes you feel any better, he was just as much of a jerk in high school."

"Good to know it's not just me."

"No." Aaron laughed. "I wanted to tell you, I put aside some new history books for you. I thought I might see you again. I'm leaving for the day now, but just ask for them. They're right near the register."

"Thanks, but I'm not sure I'm going to need them."

"Why not? Did you find what you were looking for?"

"Sort of. I was looking for information about the house I'm living in. Kensington House. I'm sure you know it."

"Oh, yeah, sure, Kensington House. Everyone knows that place. If you ask me, I always thought there was more to that story."

"What do you mean?"

"Well, history definitely hasn't been kind to William Kensington. I studied that period in time last semester, and I always thought something about what happened didn't add up."

"Really? How?"

"I mean, before Kensington offed that dude, Nathan Newbury, he seemed to have lived a quiet and upstanding life. Served his country. Seemed to be a patriot. I know there were spies in the Union army, but if Kensington was a spy, he was an awful one. Other than his interaction with Newbury, there's no evidence of him doing anything traitorous."

Something inside me relaxed. It was like I had exhaled a breath I didn't know I was holding. It wasn't really much that a kid in college had a feeling that William was a good guy, but it was *something*. And it validated what I was feeling inside. "Maybe I *will* take a look at those books you set aside for me after all," I said.

"Cool. Well, as I said, they're there whenever you want them. Have a great day!" He strode down the street.

"What a nice kid," I said to Marlena.

"I'm not surprised. I would imagine Sadie would only hire the best."

Sadie.

Aaron had said something about Sadie at the bookstore that day. How he hadn't been able to find her for a period right before Marlena's body was discovered in the bathroom. "I'll be right back," I said.

"What's the matter?"

"Um, I have to go to the bathroom."

I went inside Ye Olde Salem Book Shoppe. Sadie was at the register, talking with some patrons who had Marlena's book in their hands. It was still selling well. I tried not to think about Penelope Givens as I walked toward the back of the store, which was mostly empty. The bathroom door was closed, and there was crime scene tape across the front.

I stood there, wondering if I should attempt to open the door, when a man wearing a trench coat whisked past me.

"Excuse me," he said. He was a muscular guy in his late forties and looked like a detective from a TV show. I wondered if it was the guy Officer Callahan had mentioned. Detective Greg Daniels.

The man ignored the crime scene tape as if it weren't there and reached for the bathroom door. When he opened it, I half expected to see Marlena's body lying there, but it wasn't. (Thank God.) And whatever blood had spattered on the floor was gone, too.

The man, detective, whatever he was, only had the door open for a few seconds as he peered in, presumably looking for something, but it was enough time for me to see what I had come looking for.

In the corner of the room—under a waste basket—was that flat piece of wood I had found in my basement. The one covering a trapdoor.

Could that be another way into the bookshop bathroom? Other than the main door? Who would have access to that?

Sadie.

"Can I help you with anything?" the man said, startling me out of my reverie. The bathroom door was now closed, and he was eyeing me suspiciously. "This is a crime scene, you know."

"Yeah, I know. Sorry." I began walking toward the front of the store, feeling his eyes on me, but my mind was reeling.

What did this mean?

If there was another way to get into the bathroom, wouldn't the police know that? Hadn't they inspected the room from top to bottom during their investigation?

Sadie smiled at me as I headed toward the register. "Did you find everything you were looking for?"

"Well, actually, I think Aaron left some books for me to pick up."

Sadie searched the top of the counter. "Ah, yes, the books about Salem's history?"

"Yes, those are them."

She rang them up, and I quickly paid, glancing back at the man, detective, whatever he was, who was inspecting the hinges of the bathroom door.

"I hope you enjoy them." Sadie handed me a paper bag with the purchased books.

"Thank you," I said sheepishly and then exited the store, wondering if I had just exchanged pleasantries with Marlena Ryder's murderer.

Chapter 18

"Everything all right?" Marlena asked when I returned.

"Let's walk," I said under my breath, glancing at the security cameras above the bookstore. When we were far enough away, I motioned toward an empty bench and placed my package of books beside me.

"What is it?" Marlena asked.

"How well do you know Sadie?"

She shrugged. "Pretty well, I think. We were friends in high school. Both interested in literature, although our interests took us in different directions—me as a writer, her as a supportive literary force. In addition to running the bookstore, Sadie does all kinds of outreach for the literary community. She almost single-handedly boosted eighth grade language scores on standardized tests in Salem. Why?"

"Is it possible that she could have done this to you?" I asked.

Marlena stared at me. "Are you crazy? Sadie? Why?"

"I don't know. I thought maybe you might know."

Marlena continued staring. "Wow, I'm beginning to agree with you."

"You think she did it?"

"No, I am beginning to agree with you that you're an awful sleuth." She shook her head. "You think Ronnie—critical, judgmental Ronnie—is innocent. And yet you think Sadie—supportive, philanthropic, wonderful Sadie—might be the murderer?"

"Things aren't always as they seem."

Marlena wasn't buying it, which was ironic for a person whose author headshot was on the back cover of a book she didn't write. But no need to belabor the point. "Look, I don't know who did this to you. All I'm saying is that we need to keep an open mind."

"Is that why you went into the bookstore?"

I nodded. "I really did want to go to the bathroom. But not for the reasons you're thinking. I wanted to look around."

"Did you find anything?"

"Well, the door was closed, but some detective-looking guy needed to open it."

"That *was* a detective. I've seen him around. Daniels is his name, I think."

So, he *was* the guy that Officer Callahan had mentioned. "Daniels opened the door for some reason, and I could see in."

"So?"

"The day you were murdered, while you were in the bathroom, Sadie went missing for a time. Aaron had been looking for her and couldn't find her."

"I say again ... so? The bookstore was mobbed that day." She said the word *mobbed* with pride. "There was an event going on. Lots of people. She was probably busy."

"Yeah, but she was missing at the precise moment you were in there. Isn't that coincidental?"

Marlena waved a gray, dismissive hand. "That seems ridicu—" She stopped. Her eyes stared off.

"What?"

"I'm remembering now. She did seem to disappear. I was looking for her to ask how much time I had before the book signing, but I couldn't find her." She looked at me. "I just assumed she was busy with customers. I thought I could get into the bathroom and out before anyone missed me." She shrugged. "That didn't work out so well."

"Okay, so we have a couple of names for suspects, right? We have Ronnie, although, as I mentioned, that doesn't feel right to me."

"Yes, your seasoned sleuthing experience tells you that." She rolled her eyes.

I ignored her. "Then there's Penelope Givens, the author of the book you plagiarized."

"*Shhhhh* ... keep your voice down, please." Marlena looked around as if someone might hear our conversation.

"And now there's Sadie." How strange that only women were on the suspect list so far. Perhaps that said something about men and reading.

"Maybe she was uploading her Instagram photos at the time," Marlena offered.

"During a crowded book event?" It didn't make sense. I reached for my phone. "Taylor said the photos are on the store's Instagram feed. Isn't it weird that the photos are still available for everyone to see? Wouldn't the police want those photos down?"

Before Marlena could answer, I had a thought. "Or maybe they're there purposely. The police hope that if someone recognizes something or someone, they'll call it in. Or maybe the opposite!" I could feel myself getting excited. "They're there to make the murderer feel at ease!"

"Okay, Jessica Fletcher ..."

"No, seriously, if the murderer is somewhere in those photos, they might think the people in the photos aren't suspects and that they had gotten away with it—and might be less careful."

"Or *more* careful," she said, "if they think someone might recognize them from the photos."

My excitement deflated. "That theory works, too." I found the Instagram feed for Ye Olde Salem Book Shoppe on my phone. The last post included five photos from Marlena's book signing. All had been taken from the point of view of the stage. I zoomed into each photo, one by one. On the third one, I saw myself sitting in the back row, talking to Sebastian.

"Do you recognize any of these people?" I showed Marlena my phone.

She rolled her eyes again. "Really? I recognize practically all of them."

"Okay, maybe we need to go about this the other way. How many of these people do you *not* recognize?"

"Can you swipe and zoom for me?" Marlena said. "I haven't quite figured out the fine motor skills ghost thing."

As I swiped and zoomed, Marlena studied each photo. "There's quite a few I don't know," she said finally. "Maybe about ten or fifteen."

"Do you see Penelope Givens in the audience?"

She looked them over and shook her head. "No, but I haven't seen her in a very long time. Years. I'm not sure I would remember what she looked like."

I found that hard to believe. I would have thought the guilt from what Marlena had done would have Penelope's face haunting her for years. Enough for her to stuff that manuscript under the floorboard of her office.

"This person with the blond hair looks vaguely familiar," Marlena said, "but I can't say I know her."

I looked at the person Marlena was pointing to. The woman looked familiar to me, too. I realized it was the lady who had been sitting beside me, the one with the tattoo on her hand who had picked up her things and moved to a seat in the second row. That's when Sebastian took her seat and, well, I had forgotten all about her.

"And this gentleman here." Marlena pointed to the man who had been dressed in a suit, the only other male audience member in the room besides Sebastian. "He had asked me my favorite part of being an author."

"You remember what he asked you?"

"Well, I tend to remember what attractive men ask." I could swear she was blushing; a darker shade of gray colored Marlena's cheeks.

Hmm... "Are you sure you don't know that guy?" I asked.

"I just said I didn't."

"You weren't having an affair with him? Because if you *were*, then his wife would be a primary murder suspect."

"What makes you think I'm the kind of person to have an affair with a married man?"

Really? "Um, because a ton of love letters were found in the same hiding spot as Penelope's manuscript."

Marlena's right eyelid quivered again. "Listen, you don't know the whole story. Jacob's wife was ill, and he needed comforting."

"That's what you call it?" I pointed to the guy in the photo. "Is that Jacob?"

"No, that's not him. He moved to the West Coast."

"And what about Jacob's wife? Could she have murdered you?"

"No."

"You're sure?"

"Yes. She passed away a few years back, which is why Jacob moved. But his wife found out about the affair and confronted me. I apologized for it. It was wrong. I know that." She shook off the memory. "I don't think this is getting us anywhere."

I clicked out of Instagram and opened another window.

"What are you doing now?"

The only thing I could think of. "We need to find Penelope Givens."

Chapter 19

PENELOPE GIVENS WAS PRETTY easy to find. Even for a novice sleuth like me. Although I shouldn't have been surprised. Virtually *everybody* was pretty easy to find in these days of social media and GPS and all things internet. (And you were especially easy to find if you were dumb enough to seek refuge in the one city your sick twist of a husband was scheduled to visit for a tech conference each year. But I digress...)

The contact number Marlena had for Penelope was no longer in service, but a quick online search found an address not far from Salem. In a place called Swampscott, Massachusetts. The name *Swampscott* brought to mind a cross between the Creature from the Black Lagoon and *The Great Gatsby*. I imagined that description on the front of the town's travel brochure.

"Honestly, I don't think you need me here," Marlena said.

She had been complaining the entire walk to Swampscott. Yes, she didn't want to be here—newsflash!—but neither did I. I had planned on driving the four miles, but Marlena said she didn't trust herself not to fall through the front seat while the car was in transit. Hmmm, I didn't buy it. She had been doing pretty well with her sitting and knocking and leaning practice. I knew an excuse when I heard one. I couldn't say I blamed her, though. It wasn't every day you came face to face with the person whose intellectual property you poached.

"We're almost there," I said, adjusting my earbuds so that I could pretend to be on the phone and not gain any attention. The earbuds were old, and I lost the fuzzy covers somewhere in my backpack, but they did the trick.

I took a long, deep breath while Marlena sulked. It was nice to get my body moving again. Aside from the long walk I had taken yesterday, I hadn't been getting any regular exercise or been to the gym in months, although I hated the gym. Joe had insisted I go. "I can't have a wife with flabby thighs," he liked to say. *Jerk.* Long Island was much more of a driving place. Unless you lived near the mall or a major street, there wasn't much within walking distance. I looked forward to walking more often. Salem gave me a reason to.

"C'mon, perk up," I said. "Look at the clouds. The blue sky. It's another beautiful day."

Marlena crossed her arms. "I don't feel like talking."

"Tell me about Penelope. What does she look like?"

"I told you. It's hard to remember."

"Just some broad strokes, maybe? Is she tall? Blond?"

"No, she's a petite woman with long straight hair that she wears in a ponytail. Brown eyes, I think. Nothing really memorable."

"Ouch."

Marlena shrugged. "This might be terrible to say, but Penelope looked like she didn't have much money."

What did *that* mean? No designer jeans? No expensive haircut? No snazzy car? "Why do you say that?"

"I don't know. Her clothing. Her fingernails, which, while always clean, weren't polished. And like I said, she typed her book on a typewriter, which told me she didn't have access to a computer."

Which made her the perfect person to steal from? Ugh. Marlena was right. We were better off not talking. How did I let William talk me into helping this person?

I glanced at my GPS. One more minute till our arrival. As we crossed the street, I gazed at the tall apartment building in front of me. "I think this is it."

We were standing in front of a building complex that looked pretty new. More Gatsby, less Black Lagoon. The place looked like it had just been opened in the last few years. Signs pointed to a tennis court, an outdoor pool, and a rec center. Seemed more like a vacation rental than a place to live.

"It looks like Penelope is doing okay if she lives here." I was happy to see that. After what Marlena had done to her, I hoped that she was doing well for herself. I looked at the address on my phone. Apartment 8A. "I guess she lives on the eighth floor."

"Maybe I should wait outside," Marlena tried again.

"I think you need to do this, Marlena. If Penelope is your killer, you need to know."

"But how am I supposed to know? I didn't see the person who killed me."

"Maybe something will come to you. Maybe a certain scent of shampoo. Or way of breathing. I don't know. It's worth a try."

"And if she's not the person who killed me?"

"Then you need to face her for other reasons."

We walked toward the entrance, but the doors were locked. There was an intercom system to the side on the brick wall. "It looks like you need to be buzzed," I said when the front door opened, and a woman and a little girl no more than three years old stepped out. The little girl held the door.

"Here you go!" she said in a tiny voice.

"Why, thank you," I said as Marlena and I stepped into the building. "You're very polite."

"I hope you both have a nice day," the little girl said.

Both? *She can see Marlena?* That was the second child in the past few days who could see a ghost. Why? And why could *I* see ghosts, too?

Puzzled, the little girl's mother scrunched her eyebrows but then took her hand and walked away.

There was no one at the lobby's front desk, which was a stroke of luck. Since this was an unexpected visit, it would have been difficult to explain exactly why we were there. Well, why *I* was there.

We took the elevator to the eighth floor and walked down the hallway to 8A. I raised my hand to knock, but hesitated.

"What's the matter?" Marlena asked.

"Nothing. I just need a minute."

What was I going to say? There was a very real possibility that the person who opened the door would be the one who had murdered Marlena Ryder in cold blood. *Why am I doing this again?* I asked myself with a sigh. I could be sitting at home with my bestest-buddy Boy. Playing fetch with my old blond wig. Watching Ghost Cat weave in and out of walls. Talking to William about my favorite book. Or maybe all about his past. *At some point, we are going to have to talk about it.* Instead of being here with a murdered author and a potential murderer.

I knocked anyway.

There was a scuffling inside, and after a moment's hesitation, the door opened.

I expected to see the person Marlena had described standing there. Someone young with a long ponytail. Instead, there was a middle-aged woman wearing rubber gloves on her hands and a kerchief around her head.

"That's not Penelope," Marlena whispered.

Yeah, no kidding.

"Can I help you?" the woman asked.

"Hi, I'm looking for Penelope Givens," I said.

The woman narrowed her eyes at me. "Who are you?"

"I'm, um ... a friend of a friend." That was the best I could do without lying completely. Marlena *had* been a friend to Penelope, at least at first. Although Marlena *certainly* wasn't any friend to me. A tiny stretch of the truth on both ends. "My name is Clara Kelly."

The woman looked me up and down. And not once at Marlena, thank God. "Penelope isn't here."

"Will she be back today?"

The woman blinked a few times. "What is this regarding?"

"I just wanted to talk with her about something. I may have found something she's looking for. That she ... um, misplaced." I didn't exactly know how much to say. That I had found her manuscript under the floorboard of a dead author's home office? I wasn't even sure who this woman was. I stared into her eyes. They were brown. Hadn't Marlena said that Penelope's eyes were brown? I took a chance. "Are you ... her mother?"

A pause. "Yes." She said the words with no emotion. Or maybe in a way that was trying to stifle emotion. There was something about the woman that seemed defeated, broken. I was getting a weird vibe. "I'm afraid I can't help you," she said and went to close the door.

"Wait!" I called, and the door opened slightly. "When you see her, can you tell her—"

"I don't get to see her as much as I would like," her mother said. "I have to work. I don't have much free time."

"I don't understand," I said, confused. "Does Penelope live here?"

The mother was losing patience, it seemed. "No. Not for a long time."

"Would you be able to tell me where she is? I'd really like to speak with her. It's important."

The woman took a deep breath. "You're a friend, you say? You do look familiar."

"Well, a friend of a friend."

"Penelope is in Boston Medical Center. In the in-patient psych ward. Where she's been for the last six months." And with that, she closed the door.

Chapter 20

Plot twist.

"Well, it looks like Penelope Givens is no longer a suspect," I said to Marlena as we left the apartment building. "Where does that leave us now?" Narrowing down the suspect list definitely should have felt like a step forward, but somehow it felt like a step back.

"Don't be so sure," Marlena said. "We don't know the circumstances surrounding Penelope's situation."

"What do you mean? Her mother said she has been there for six months."

"She's been *living* there for six months. But if she admitted herself, it's possible that she could have left the hospital whenever she would have liked." Marlena's gray eyes grew wide. I found it interesting that Marlena's eyes had no real color to them, unlike William's eyes, which were such a vivid pale blue. "Maybe she signed herself out to commit my murder and then went back. Maybe that was her plan. I mean, if she's already a crazy person, then we're halfway there. Now that I think about it, she did look a bit desperate when I saw her last."

I was beginning to think Marlena's lack of eye color was due to her lack of empathy. William had more empathy in his gray pinkie than she did in her entire body. But she did have a point. We didn't know much about why Penelope had been hospitalized, and her mother didn't seem inclined to offer up any information. Not that she should to a couple of strangers who showed up at her door. Well, *one* stranger.

"Well, now at least it makes sense as to why she dropped off the face of the earth after she gave me her manuscript," Marlena said. "She was ill."

"Yeah, but her mother said she had only been in the hospital for six months. When did she give you the manuscript?"

"Oh, gosh ..." Marlena's eyes rolled up as if she were consulting a mental calendar. "A couple of years ago, maybe?"

"We need to find out more. At this point, we have more questions than answers." I stuck my earbuds back into my ears, and we started walking back. "Maybe we should visit her."

Marlena stopped walking. "At the hospital? You can't be serious."

"I am absolutely serious. Why?"

"I ... I just can't go there. Psych wards give me the willies. There are violent people there."

"Marlena, you're a thriller author. All you write about is violence and stuff."

"Yes, I'm brave on paper. Kind of a weenie in real life."

So much of a weenie that she would steal someone's book instead of writing her own. "Well, I'd like to visit her. You're right. There is a possibility she could have left the hospital. But there's another reason I need to go. Penelope really needs to know the truth about her book. That she has written a bestseller."

"What good will that do? The manuscript you found doesn't really prove anything. Not in the eyes of the law. Anybody can type up my book, plop in a few different names, and claim they wrote it."

"That may be true. But even if nobody else knew, I need Penelope to know. That she really did write the book. That she has talent. Maybe that will help her."

The walk back to Salem seemed to take longer than the walk to Swampscott. I was dragging a little, and Marlena was quiet. Finally, when we made it back to Kensington House, she said, "I just can't go with you to Boston Medical Center."

"I think you'll be okay in the car, Marlena. We'll go tomorrow morning. Bright and early. That will give you the rest of the day to practice sitting."

"It's not that. I just can't—"

Chapter 21

I couldn't sleep. *Again.* All sorts of people filled my mind. Penelope Givens. Penelope's mother. Detective Daniels. Sadie. Ronnie. Marlena. And, of course, William.

I had to smile, though. Not one of those names belonged to Joe. For eight years, *all* I thought about was Joe. Getting away from him. I may have had bloodshot eyes, but this was progress.

Beside me, Boy was letting out tiny snores. At least one of us was sleeping soundly.

I reached over to the nightstand and picked up one of the books I had bought at Sadie's book shop. *Notorious Figures in New England History.* One of the books the librarian had also recommended. I opened to a page I had bookmarked, one that talked about William. There was some additional information about him. More than the book I found at the library. I reread the passage I underlined.

William Kensington's name may not be widely known to the general American populace, but it is a name associated with shame to those familiar with New England history. Known as a boot and shoe maker, he joined the Union army during the Civil War and was convicted of treason and sentenced to death for the brutal stabbing death of Union army hero Nathan Newbury, an esteemed soldier of the Union army.

Brutal.

The word stood out.

It was hard to associate it with the ghost I was living with.

I thought about Marlena. How death might be changing her. How she seemed to have a change of heart about what she had done to Penelope. And about having an affair. Had the same happened to William? Had he been this *brutal* person when he was alive and then understood the error of his ways as a ghost?

The book had a little bit more information about Nathan Newbury as well. Newbury was apparently about to marry when he was stabbed by William.

Newbury served the Union army honorably since the commencement of the Civil War and comes from a long line of distinguished statesmen and military leaders. His death came as a blow to the Union and, in particular, his hometown of Salem, which erected a monument in his memory.

I averted my eyes from the page. The more I read, the worse it got. I put the book down and turned off the light, snuggling next to Boy and tracing his curly black-and-white tail with my finger.

Tomorrow, I'll visit Penelope Givens. Tell her I know what Marlena did and return her book to its rightful owner. Give her some good news. Because after the few days I've had, I could use a little good news myself.

Chapter 22

It was weird being in Boston. For two reasons. 1) Even though it's only a half hour's drive from Salem, the vibe is so different. More city, less small town. And 2) it was nearly impossible to come here and not think of Joe. The only time he wanted me to travel with him was when I "accompanied" him to the annual tech conference in Boston. At least that's what he called it. *Accompany*. Meanwhile, I didn't accompany him *anywhere*. I barely left the hotel room.

I shook my head, ridding my mind of his image. I would not let Joe haunt me. He may have found a way to seep into my dreams, but I wouldn't let him occupy my thoughts while I was awake.

I parked my car in the indoor garage of Boston Medical Center and made my way inside. The man at the front door directed me to the psychiatric side of the hospital, and after getting through security, I approached a set of desks and asked to visit Penelope Givens.

"Are you a friend?" the woman working there asked. She had pretty, but weary eyes, as if she was already in the middle of a long day, even though it was only morning.

Friend? How had I referred to myself to Penelope's mother? "I'm a friend of a friend," I said, clutching Penelope's book in my hands.

"Penelope doesn't get many visitors," the woman said with a tired smile. "And she never leaves, so this will be a nice surprise."

"She doesn't leave the hospital?"

The woman shook her head. "Not once in six months."

If that's so, then Penelope Givens, for sure, didn't murder Marlena.

The woman handed me a visitor's pass. "Right that way," she pointed. "Room 17A."

A buzzer sounded. Locks unlatched. I felt like I was in an episode of *Oz*. Then a door opened, and I walked into a room filled with individuals—mostly young people—milling around, a blank look in their eyes. If I didn't know any better, I would have thought I had walked onto a college campus during finals week. I stuck my visitor's pass onto my shirt and looked for Room 17A.

As I read the ascending door numbers, my heart began beating faster. What would I say? How should I broach the topic of Marlena? It wasn't every day someone returned the novel you wrote that was stolen from you.

Room 17A was at the end of the hallway. When I got there, I peered inside, but it was empty.

"Can I help you?" a voice said from behind me. I turned around.

I didn't know what I was expecting, but the only word that came to mind when I saw Penelope Givens sitting near the window, on top of a radiator, was *sad*. She had a long ponytail like Marlena described, but her hair looked unwashed and uncared for. Her eyes were puffy with dark circles, and she was wearing a hoodie with no drawstring and sneakers with no laces. She was holding an open book in her hands, and I tried not to think of the open book lying on top of Marlena's dead body.

"Hi, Penelope. I'm Clara Kelly."

"Do I know you?" She closed her book.

As I got closer, my initial reaction started to fade. Underneath the unkempt exterior, Penelope had a kind face. Expressive eyes. An upturned mouth. A calm demeanor. She may have been medicated, but she didn't appear to my amateur-sleuth mind to be a murderer.

"No, you don't know me," I said. "I went to visit your home yesterday and spoke to your mother. She said you were here."

She looked at me. "So, I don't know you?"

"Would you like me to leave?"

She shook her head. "No. Do you know you're the first visitor I've ever had? Other than my mother. Do you want me to get you a chair?"

I sat down on the radiator. "No, this is fine."

"I had lots of friends once, but those relationships didn't last. We moved around a lot when I was growing up." She rocked a little. I wasn't sure how old Penelope was, but she couldn't be more than twenty-five, although she seemed younger. "My mother lost her job about two years ago. We were on the streets. Homeless. It's hard to keep relationships when you don't have a place to call home."

"I'm so sorry. Is that why you're here? It must have been difficult."

"Believe it or not, I was weathering that period of my life well. My mom and I tend to persevere. We just put our heads down and do what we have to do. I know she wishes she could visit me more. But she has to work in order to afford this place." She motioned to the room.

"Why are you here then?"

Sadness filled her big eyes. "It all had to do with a book."

My fingers tensed around the package in my hands.

"I had written a book," Penelope continued. "Sounds great, right? I was so proud of it. I brought it to a local writers' workshop in Salem, which is where we lived for a good while. One of the writers there worked as an editor, and I thought she might be able to help me. We both wrote the same genre. I gave her my book, but then we lost our apartment, and we had to try and find another place to live. It was tough."

"I'm so sorry to hear that."

"My mother, though, is amazing. She cleans houses. *Really* well. She's a perfectionist. And slowly but surely, she developed a reputation. I found odd jobs where I could. But we had to lose most of our possessions. The only thing I had of value was my grandfather's typewriter, but I ended up selling it. And not for much." She looked up at me. "I'm sure you don't want to hear all this."

"No, I'd love to hear it."

"It's nice to talk to someone new." She gave a small smile. "Finally, my mother began working for a woman in Swampscott. And she became a good customer. This client loved my mother's work so much that when her husband got transferred to Sweden for a couple of years, she said my mother—and me too—could stay in the apartment while they were gone. If we could take in the mail. And water the plants. It was the kindest gesture. So, that's where we're living now. They have a lot of money. And they pay my mother well. It's helped pay for health insurance for both of us. And it's really helped us get on our feet and save a little money. We are tremendously indebted to her."

"That's amazing."

"It is. It's allowing us to save up some money and get a place of our own one day. When we got settled in the apartment, I kept visiting the writers' workshop, hoping I could run into the author—her name is Marlena Ryder—and retrieve my book. But I couldn't find her. Someone told me she moved away. To New York City. I looked for her on social media, but she never responded to my messages. Then one morning, about six months ago, I was walking home from a new job as a staff writer for a website when I saw a billboard." Her shoulders sagged. "A billboard for the newest book that was being hailed as the book of the summer."

Goosebumps shot up my arms. I anticipated the words as they rolled off her tongue.

"*The Secrets We Keep*," Penelope said. "By ... Marlena Ryder. I didn't really have money to buy her book, but the local library had it. I started to read it." Her eyes welled with tears. "I know this sounds crazy, but ... it was *my* book." She shook her head. "Right there. A few words had been changed, but it was my book."

"What did you do?"

"I didn't know *what* to do. I didn't think anyone would believe me, and I just kinda shut down after that. My mom was so worried about me. She suggested I check myself in here, and this is where I've been cocooning. I know I can't stay here forever. I thought I would lose my job, but my editor said it would be waiting for me when I got out of here. Isn't that nice? Although I'm sure he won't wait indefinitely."

"Was that the only copy of the book you had? The one you gave her?"

She nodded. "Yes. Besides the one I mailed to myself. It took me forever to type up that whole book again."

"Mailed to yourself?"

"They say to do that. Mail something to yourself and not open the package in order to prove copyright. But I don't know what happened to the package when we lost our apartment."

I shook my head. What Marlena had done was worse than simply stealing. It had devastated this young woman and put a financial burden on her and her mother. And set Penelope's literary career back years—possibly forever.

"I thought things couldn't get any worse," she said, "and then I heard."

"Heard what?"

"That the author—Marlena Ryder—had been killed."

I watched her closely. "Why did that make it worse?"

"Because it's something I had dreamt about for a long time. Harming her. For what she did. And then when she was murdered, I felt guilty for thinking that. I mean, it's just a book, right? You have to look at the big picture. And besides, her death does me more harm than good."

"Why?"

"Because now there's no one else who knows the truth."

I held up the envelope on my lap. "That's not true."

"What do you mean?"

"I have something to show you." I reached into the envelope and pulled out Penelope's manuscript.

Penelope stared at the looseleaf binder in my hands. At her own handwriting on the front cover. "Where did you get this?"

"The woman who moved into Marlena's home in Salem gave it to me. She found it underneath the floorboards in her home office. It's the book you gave to Marlena. Your *best-selling* book."

Penelope reached for the binder, and I gave it to her. "I always wondered how I would feel if I saw this again. You know, I started to think I was crazy. That maybe I *hadn't* really written the book."

How ironic. Over time, Marlena started to believe that she *had* written it. "You did write it. And you deserve to get credit for it."

Penelope tried to hand the binder back to me. "I appreciate the effort. But I'm not sure this helps me. Anybody can claim they wrote any book."

"But what about the copy you mailed to yourself? That's real proof."

She shrugged. "Lost in the mail, I guess."

"You should keep this, though. Maybe you'll figure out a way to prove that you're the author. I can help you." I looked at my watch. "But I'm afraid I have to get going. I have an appointment this afternoon. But I'll leave this with you. It's been apart from you for too long. And I wrote my phone number on the outside of this envelope." I handed her the envelope. "If you want to talk again, please call me."

"You are very kind," she said. "You didn't have to come all this way."

I nodded, thinking that now was probably not a good time to say I had also come to see for myself if she had murdered Marlena Ryder. As I got up and walked down the corridor, I glanced back. Penelope was staring down at the looseleaf binder, her fingers tracing her handwriting on the cover. Her shoulders still hung heavy, but for the first time since I'd been there, a small smile appeared on her face.

I wanted to believe it was a sign of hope.

As I'd learned, hope was all you needed to change your life.

Chapter 23

THE SALEM POLICE DEPARTMENT was housed in a freestanding building on Margin Street, not far from Kensington House. Another example of how everything was within walking distance in Salem. At this rate, my legs would be toned in a few months. I parked the car in my driveway and walked the short distance.

Inside the building, a few police officers were standing around. At the far end of the room, Officer Callahan looked like he was chatting up a female officer. I could see him flexing the muscles in his arms from here. When he noticed me, he unflexed and walked over.

"Why, Mrs. Kelly, so nice to see you." He looked around the room.

"What are you looking for?" I asked.

"Well, I'm just surprised. I don't see any dead bodies around you at the moment." He looked at his watch. "Maybe I'm early."

"Very funny, Officer Callahan." Apparently, he had a dark sense of humor. I kinda liked that. I much preferred when a person's darkness was out in the open. "Please call me Clara." I didn't know how much longer I could deal with the *Mrs. Kelly* stuff.

Callahan smiled, his white raccoon eyes squinting on his suntanned face. "How can I help you today, Clara?"

Thank God. "Well, Detective Daniels asked me to come in. I'm not sure why."

The smile on Callahan's face disappeared. I hoped it was because Daniels wasn't Officer Callahan's favorite subject and not because of the reason I had been called to the precinct. "Right this way, Mrs. Kelly ... I mean, Clara."

Callahan escorted me through a metal detector and then down a long hallway. "Do you know what this is about, Officer Callahan?"

"Daniels is asking some of the people who were in the bookstore the day of Marlena Ryder's murder to come in for additional questioning." He pointed to a bench in front of a closed door. "You can wait right here."

"Thank you." As I watched Callahan walk back toward the lobby of the precinct, the door to the room in front of me opened, and a gentleman exited. I recognized him as the man who had attended Marlena's book signing. The man

Marlena claimed *not* to have an affair with. He had a suit on again today. He nodded at me and walked in the same direction as Callahan.

"And you are?"

Detective Daniels stepped out of the room. He looked more imposing without so many books around him. Even though he was about average height, probably in his late forties, he was muscular in a way that looked like he wasn't really trying. He also had very white teeth. *Too* white. I could see why Callahan liked to wear sunglasses.

"You look familiar," Daniels said to me.

"Yeah, we ran into each other at Ye Olde Salem Book Shoppe. By the bathroom. I'm Clara Kelly."

"Ah, yes. That's right." He looked at me suspiciously, as if I were a murderer who had gone back to the scene of her crime. "Well, go on in. Detective Morris will get you situated. I've gotta hit the head."

Charming.

I walked into the small room where a petite woman was fiddling with a recorder of some kind. There was a small TV screen on the table, along with what looked like an old-fashioned VCR below it.

"Have a seat, Ms. Kelly," she said.

By the time I sat in the chair, Daniels was back and closed the door. I suddenly felt like I was trapped in a cage with a tiger. "Thank you for coming in," he said, taking the seat next to Detective Morris.

I prepared myself for the Good Cop/Bad Cop routine. Maybe I had seen one too many episodes of *Law & Order.* "Sure, how can I help you?" I asked.

"This is in regard to the investigation of the murder of Marlena Ryder," he said.

I nodded. "How is the investigation going?"

"We don't really discuss that." Daniels shuffled some papers in front of him, probably trying to look important. He was all business and then directed my attention to the monitor on the table. "From what we can tell, everyone who entered Ye Olde Salem Book Shoppe between the time it opened at ten a.m. and the time the Salem police led everyone out through the exits has been accounted for. In other words, everyone who went in, went out at some point after."

I thought of the trapdoor in the bathroom. "Unless the killer was already in the bookshop before it opened."

Daniels and Morris stared at me like I was a fly in their investigative ointment.

Keep quiet, I told myself, *and let them take the lead.* This sleuthing was getting to my head. No reason to have them suspect me more than they needed to.

"As I was saying," Daniels consulted a paper on the desk, "you entered the bookshop at exactly eleven fifty-eight a.m."

"That's correct."

"That was a statement, not a question." Daniels glanced again at Morris.

"Oh, sorry."

Daniels rewound the video to the precise moment I entered the bookshop and paused. The point of view of the image was from inside the store, above the register, and not from the streetlamp outside. "That is you, correct, Ms. Kelly?"

"Yes."

"Is it me, Ms. Kelly, or do you look a little concerned?"

"Concerned?"

"Yes, you seemed to have walked into the bookshop like a woman on a mission. You don't look as excited as the others to be there."

He stared at me, but I said nothing.

"Well?" he asked.

"Oh, sorry. I thought that was a statement, not a question."

Daniels narrowed his eyes. "Why did you go to the bookshop that day? Were you a fan of the author's?"

I shook my head. "I had never heard of her before. I wasn't there to see her."

"Well, then, why were you there?" Daniels asked.

"I was there to get some books about the history of the house I just moved into."

"Ah, yes." Daniels pulled a sheet of paper from a stack and read off my address. "That is your current address, yes?"

"Yes."

"Kensington House, as it's called, correct?"

"Yes."

I thought he might ask me why I was looking for local history books, but it seemed Daniels was just as familiar with the house I had moved into as everyone else in Salem. Instead, he fast-forwarded the video a bit and stopped. "Do you know this woman?" he asked. "She is one of the few people we have been unable to identify."

On the screen was a woman with blond hair. I recognized the interesting tattoo on the back of her hand—a geometric pattern with ovals. "Yes, I do. I don't know her name. She was sitting next to me."

Daniels scrunched his eyebrows, as if perplexed. "Are you sure?"

My body tensed. Joe always asked me if I was sure. It made me doubt everything I said. "Yes, I'm sure."

He fast-forwarded the video, and I watched the blond woman speed-walk to the front desk, pick up three copies of *The Secrets We Keep*, and move out of frame. Then Daniels stopped the video and opened the folder in front of him. It was filled with papers and photos. He plucked one out and pushed it toward me. One of Sadie's photos that I had seen on Instagram. He pointed to me sitting in the back.

"This is you, correct?" he asked.

"Correct."

He pointed to Sebastian sitting next to me. "This is not a blond woman." He moved his finger several rows in front of me and pointed to her. "She is here. It seems to me you are mistaken."

Boy, this guy is really smug. "I'm not mistaken. She had been sitting next to me but then moved closer to the stage when a seat became available. Sebastian," I pointed to the photo, "took her seat after she moved."

"Bartender?" he asked.

"Pet groomer," I said, but I had a feeling he already knew that.

Daniels let out a quick sigh and then sat back in his seat. He fast-forwarded the video, and that's when I saw Sadie. She was at the front of the store. Bending down to help a little girl who was crying. I looked at the time on the video. It was right when Aaron was looking for her, between Marlena's book talk and the beginning of the book signing.

So *that* was why Aaron and Marlena couldn't find her when they were looking for her. Sadie was bending down to help a little girl in a crowd of people. She was innocent.

Detective Daniels kept fast-forwarding until I saw myself talking to Officer Callahan and then leaving the bookshop. "And here you are leaving the store at exactly three forty-seven p.m."

"Wait, can you run that back?" I asked.

"Why?" Detective Daniels asked.

"I think I saw something."

The detectives smirked at one another. They probably couldn't fathom how someone like me—with zero training—could see something that they couldn't. They also probably didn't like the idea of being upstaged. But I had a feeling they'd humor me, if only for the opportunity to rub my face in my error. "May I?" I asked, reaching toward the video player.

Daniels crossed his arms and leaned back. "Be my guest."

I rewound the video slowly and watched myself walk backward and out of the frame. Then lots of other people were walking backward into the store. I stopped the video.

"Look," I said, pointing to the blond woman, the one they had been asking about.

"What about her?" Daniels asked.

"Look at what she's carrying. Two books." I pointed to her tattooed hand.

"So?" Daniels asked.

"So, she had *three* books when she sat next to me. And if you check the video of when she first arrived, when she walked to the register, she purchased *three* copies of *The Secrets We Keep*. Not two."

I finally had Detective Daniels's attention. He leaned forward in his chair, reached out, and rewound the video to when the blond woman entered the bookshop. He brought his face closer to the screen.

"See?" I said, not wanting to boast, but I was pretty darn proud of myself. "She's buying three books. And I remember seeing her with three books when she sat down next to me. And yet she's only leaving with two."

"Why do you think that's significant?" Detective Morris asked me.

"Because. I got a good look at the body in the bathroom. Marlena's body. I was one of the few people near that section of the store. I saw that there was a copy of her book on top of her body. If that blond woman bought three books and left with two, maybe the missing book is the one on the body."

"What do you do for a living, Ms. Kelly?" Detective Daniels asked.

Well, *that* was a sharp change in subject. "Um, I used to work in hotel management, and I'm in the process of opening my own bed-and-breakfast."

Detective Daniels was looking at a sheet of paper. "I understand your husband had an accident recently."

What did *that* have to do with anything? And what was he looking at? Did Daniels have a file on me? "Yes, he did. He fell down the stairs. A few months ago." I was trying so hard to leave Joe in my past, but how could I when his name kept being brought up? I changed the subject. "Do you think I'm right? About the book?"

Daniels closed the file. "Why don't you leave the police work to us, Ms. Kelly?"

"But—"

"It's circumstantial at best," Detective Daniels tut-tutted, organizing his paperwork.

I smiled inwardly. I knew he was lying. I could see it on his face. I was onto something. And as he handed me his card and told me to reach out if I thought of anything else, I knew that he and Detective Morris were going to rewatch the video to confirm I was right. Maybe they would check to see if any other patrons had left with fewer books than they had purchased.

"Thank you for your time," Detective Daniels said with a nod, an indication that I should go.

Thank *you*, I wanted to say.

Why? Because there was a very good possibility that I was free!

By coming here, I had stumbled upon Marlena's killer. It wasn't Penelope. It wasn't Sadie. Or Ronnie. It was an as-of-yet unidentified blond woman with an interesting tattoo on the back of her left hand—a pretty solid distinguishing characteristic.

I walked out of the station, relieved. I could let the police detectives figure out the rest. Marlena's case could be off my hands, and I could move on to other matters. Like William's past. And my future business.

I stopped walking. *Who was I kidding?* Marlena would never let me stop. I would just have to put my foot down. She'd have to understand. Salem was a small town, but there was *no way* I was going to find a blond woman with an interesting tattoo.

And if I was okay with that, she needed to be.

Chapter 24

I walked into Kensington House, with Boy in tow, and almost walked out, thinking I was in the wrong place. I barely recognized it. Many of the walls had been opened, the depths of their insides on display, plaster on the floor in pieces. The plumber had left pipes—old ones, new ones—lying around like Lincoln Logs. If a house had private parts, I was gazing at them and had the impulse to cover my eyes.

Bark!

Boy was pulling on his leash, eager to check out the carnage. I'm sure there were all kinds of smells he needed to investigate.

"Sorry, little fella. Looks like you're sticking with me while these walls are open."

I picked him up and carried him into the living room, then upstairs into the bedroom, and into the *secret rooms*, as I still called them, even though they weren't so secret anymore. Just about every wall had some kind of hole in it. If you had to break a few eggs to make an omelet, I had broken dozens.

"William, are you here?"

He appeared in the bedroom. "Yes."

"Was it awful?" I asked. "All the noise?"

William shrugged. "Not terrible."

Polite, as always. Meanwhile, it must have sounded like he was living in the middle of a quarry. Strangers were tearing apart the place he had called home for more than a hundred fifty years, and it was all my fault. "I'm so sorry."

"Pray, do not be. It was far more harrowing for me to witness the conduct of my grandsons and great-grandsons. This," he motioned to the walls, "is simply scenery. A means for the better." He straightened his military jacket. "Why did you come? I believed you would not be stopping by today."

"Well, I had a thought."

"Oh?"

"I thought you might like to come and spend the night at the hotel with us. Right, Boy?"

Bark! The dog wriggled in my hands.

"The hotel?" he asked.

"Yeah, you know, like a sleepover. You shouldn't have to stay in this house with it looking like this."

There was a tiny gleam in William's pale blue eyes. I wasn't sure if it was excitement or fear.

"You have never before requested my company on an outing," he said.

Guilt. Covering me like a coat. Had William been waiting for me to ask him to join us all this time? Ugh. Of course he had. He was the consummate gentleman. How could I have been so callous? "That's my fault. Not yours." I shrugged. "When I first came here, I guess I wanted so badly to be my own person that I had forgotten being on my own and being alone are two different things. You're my friend, William. My *best* friend." I smiled at him. I wasn't sure if there was such a thing as a best friend in the 1800s, but I had a feeling he would be able to figure out what the term meant even if there wasn't. "And I'd love your company for the evening."

William looked at the floor, unsure.

"C'mon, it'll be fun," I said. "You should get out of the house more often." I was *this close* to saying Vitamin D was good for the body. Some best friend I was.

"Are you assured you won't mind?" he asked. "When you first arrived, you seemed uncertain about being seen with me. I do not wish to be a burden."

Ugh. More guilt. "I was uncertain about a lot of things. But I can honestly say, right now, that you are the first ghost I'd be *happy* to walk the streets of Salem with. I truly mean that."

The corners of William's lips curved upward. Like Penelope's. A good sign. And probably the only one I would get. "C'mon, let's go."

I headed for the door confidently, not knowing if William would be behind me, but there he was. Ready for an overnight adventure. No need for a change of clothing. Or a toothbrush. One of the perks of being a ghost.

Outside, the sun was setting, and with the summer months nearly here, it was a beautiful evening—no humidity and a soft breeze to blow through the strands of our hair. Well, *my* hair. William's hair would have stayed perfectly in place during a monsoon.

"It's lovely outside, isn't it?" I said, placing Boy on the ground.

"It seems so." As we walked, I tried to imagine what it would feel like to watch the world change from day to day, year to year, from a window and not really be able to participate in it.

William and I had more in common than I thought.

He was observing everything around us. Buildings. Cars. People. Meanwhile, I couldn't stop myself from looking at William's neck to see if there were any rope marks indicating that he had been hanged. I didn't see any. Marlena didn't have any injury marks, either. I guessed ghosts only carried those horrors on the inside, where no one else could see.

"What did it look like when you lived here? Salem?" I asked, putting my earbuds in, just in case Taylor popped up. He always seemed to.

"Why do you wear those devices in your ears?"

"It's so people think I'm talking on the phone and not to myself. A little trick that seems to work well. Remember, in public spaces, I have to be mindful of appearances."

"Ah, yes." He looked around. "Salem looks different. It's grown. More like a city than the quaint little town I once knew. The more I take in, the more I reckon I didn't quite cherish it enough when I was ... among the living."

"None of us appreciate anything enough while we're among the living. Until we don't have those things anymore." I thought of my parents. "I wouldn't hold that against yourself, though. That's just what made you human."

Boy tugged on the leash, pulling me around the corner, which was the way to the hotel. It amazed me how he knew his way around Salem better than I did. He looked so proud walking with William and me, his little black-and-white curly tail tightly wound and high in the air. I directed him in a different direction. I was feeling untethered. No longer weighed down by a murder investigation. "We're taking the long way today, Boy. The scenic route. If that's all right with you, William."

"That's just fine."

We walked toward the town hall, where large groups of people were standing around.

"What brings those folks over yonder?" William asked. "Is there a town meeting?"

"Those are walking tours. You must have heard them come by the house over the years. People learn about the history of Salem. You know, *you* would be great at giving one of those tours. Put these tour guides to shame."

"Should they be shameful?"

"No, that's just an expression." I smiled. "When the bed-and-breakfast opens, it will be so great to have you with me to help me give guests a sense of what Salem was like around the time you lived in Kensington House."

"Kensington House?"

"That's what they call your house."

"Who calls it that?"

"Well, the historical society, I guess. It's pretty well known." I wished I hadn't said that because then William asked, "Well known how?"

Before I could figure out what to say, a voice interrupted my thoughts.

"Well, well, well, if it isn't Clara Kelly walking around the neighborhood, talking to herself."

Taylor from the *Salem Chronicle* was sitting on a bench with his notepad in hand. This guy seriously made a habit of turning up everywhere. Yes, it was the hallmark of a good reporter, but it was also kind of annoying. He was writing on his notepad, and I wondered how his investigation was going. Did he know about the blond woman with the tattoo on her hand? Had he had any additional contact with the Salem Police Department? Officer Callahan? Detective Daniels?

"Hi, Taylor." I pointed to my earbuds. "Sorry, I'm on the phone."

"You always seem to be on your phone. You must be a very important person." He smirked.

"Have a nice night, Taylor."

I could feel him watching me as William and I passed. Even Boy picked up the pace like he wanted nothing to do with Taylor.

"Who is that young man?" William asked. "Is he a friend of yours?"

"That's Taylor Hampton. He works at the local newspaper, the *Salem Chronicle*, and, no—definitely no—he's no friend of mine."

Soon, we came upon a walking tour, this one in front of a building with a red brick front and resembling a bank. The group was being led by a woman wearing a beret, and I realized it was Stephanie of Triple H Touring Company.

"This is the Joshua Ward House," Stephanie was saying. "It was built in 1784 by a wealthy sea merchant named, not surprisingly, Joshua Ward. It was one of the first houses in Salem to be constructed entirely of bricks."

"George Washington visited this home," William said as we passed by.

"Really?" I asked.

"Really!" Stephanie gushed. "It *was* one of the first brick houses." She furrowed her eyebrows. "Hey, we've met before, haven't we? Clara, right?"

"Yes, you've got a great memory." I wasn't sure how many people walked into Triple H Touring, but it had to be a sizable number.

"Yes, I never forget a name. It's one of my superpowers. Did you know, Clara, that George Washington paid a visit to this home right here?"

"Yeah," I glanced at William, "I've heard that before."

"Well," she directed her attention back to the group, "if you look at the second-floor window, you'll see a bust of George Washington."

"You're in good hands!" I called to the tourists as they oohed and ahhhed and snapped selfies.

Stephanie waved as we walked away.

"Is she a friend of yours?" William asked.

I shrugged. "Not really. I don't have many friends." I looked back at Stephanie. "But maybe one day. See, William? You could be running these tours. ... William?" He was looking back at Joshua House. "What is it? Do you see something?"

"Before Mr. Ward built his home there, the property was owned by a Mr. George Corwin." He wrinkled his nose. "He was not a nice man."

George Corwin. I knew the name. "Wasn't he the one who oversaw the Salem Witch Trials?"

"Yes."

I wondered for a moment if the poor souls who had been killed during the Salem Witch Trials might be haunting the area. I hoped not. I hoped their souls had been laid to rest when the Salem "witches" had been exonerated years later. Power made people do horrible things.

"Is that ice cream?" William asked suddenly, pointing to an ice cream truck and a man handing a tall chocolate cone to a child.

"Yes, it is."

William smiled a real smile. From ear to ear. "I remember it well."

Ice cream.

Releasing dopamine across the centuries.

"C'mon, let's head this way," I said, and we walked until the sun went down, Boy leading the way.

Chapter 25

Boy yelped with eagerness when we got to the hotel room. I unclipped his leash, and he ran toward the corner of the room, near the air conditioner, where I had placed his little bed. He picked up his woolly mammoth, one of several toys I brought with us for our brief stay, and curled up on the bed, gnawing on it.

"Well, this is it, our home away from home," I said to William, putting my hands in the air. "Hopefully, Kensington House will have electricity soon, and I won't have to pull drinks out of a mini fridge and pay a fortune every time I'm thirsty." I smiled.

William stood at the door, as if he didn't know what to do. He appeared uncomfortable.

"What's the matter?" I asked.

"I am unaccustomed to being in a bedroom with a woman to whom I am not wed."

"Oh, right. I know, but, really, it's totally fine. We're friends, right?"

Wiliam nodded.

"Friends do this kind of thing all the time now. You can use that bed there. See? You, me, and Boy each have our own bed." I knew William didn't sleep and didn't need a bed, but I thought he'd feel better about having his own bed, even if it went unused.

William ran his fingers along the floral-patterned duvet and then sat on a chair at the end of the room. As I turned off the air conditioner (it was totally unnecessary with a ghost nearby) and zipped open my luggage to pull out some pajamas, he said, "The last time I stayed at an inn, I was with my wife."

I froze, my yoga pants dangling from my hand. William was bringing up something from the past. All on his own. I didn't know what to say. Did I ask questions? Delve deeper? Keep it light? Clearly, this wasn't the topic I was hoping to discuss. I wanted to know about the murder. The hanging. The *treason*. But at this point, I would take anything. "Did you have a good stay?" I asked. "At the inn, I mean?"

He didn't answer the question. Instead, he eyed me curiously. "Clara, is there something weighing on your mind?"

Yes. "Um, what makes you say that?"

He exhaled deeply and soundlessly as he kept his eyes on me, reminding me of a parent becoming frustrated with a stalling child. (Technically, since William had been born in the 1800s, he could have been my parent many times over.) "Are you certain there is nothing you wish to discuss?"

"All right, there *is* something on my mind. But, just so you know, I didn't bring you here to talk about it. I wanted you here so you could have some company for the evening. I had absolutely no intention of bringing this up until you were ready to talk about it, and if you were *never* ready to talk about it, that was okay, too."

Yes, I was rambling. Even Boy knew it. He stopped gnawing on Woolly Mammoth's tusks to look at me, as if to say, *Just get on with it*. Meanwhile, William was waiting patiently.

"And I would really like to talk about it," I said, "but I'm not sure that you will."

"Well, the only way to know is to ask."

"What about Rule Number Four?"

William looked around. "No Ground Rules are posted here."

My breath hitched. Was this a loophole? Out of sight, out of mind? Sometimes new environments made people feel different. Maybe the walk here had rendered William untethered, daring, and free, too. Whatever the reason, I needed to take advantage of the opportunity, and yet, I found myself at a loss for words. "Well ..."

As much as I wanted to get to the bottom of things, I didn't want to hurt my friend. He seemed sad enough. Where to start? The beginning? I sat down on the bed and placed my yoga pants next to me. "Okay, well, I thought it might be a good idea to get one of those little plaques on the side of the house."

"Plaque?"

"Yeah, it's like a little sign that notes the year your home was built. Mr. Wiggins next door suggested I go to the historical society and get one, and that's when ..." Mavis's smug face came to mind.

"That's when?"

"A woman there asked me if I was sure about wanting one of those."

"I don't understand."

"She said she didn't think I'd want to publicize the history of our house. Well, *your* house, I mean."

William got quiet. "Clara, what is it you would like to know?"

"Well ..." *Just say it.* "Her comment got me curious. And when I was at the library with Marlena, I did a bit of research ..." Ugh. *Research* was such a cold, detached word, like I was performing a background check on my friend. But that was exactly what I was doing, wasn't it? "Is it true that you were ... hanged?"

Silence.

The worst possible answer. A non-answer.

William stared at me—or, rather, *through* me. As if looking back in time.

I immediately wanted to take back the words. Grab my yoga pants, change, and put on cartoons for William and me to watch. Who was I to ask such personal questions? "I'm sorry, William. You don't need to talk about this." This was cruel. I was making William relive something to satisfy my own morbid curiosity.

"No, no, it's all right, Clara. You are correct. We are friends. And friends should be able to confide in one another. Although I never really had such a friend. Only my wife. But if I expect you to talk to me, the courteous thing is to be able to talk to you as well."

William had no friends? I would have found that statement sad if I hadn't found it relatable. The increasing similarities between William and me were starting to freak me out. I leaned back against the bed's headboard and pulled my legs under me. "But only if you want to talk," I said.

"Strangely, I do. I thought never speaking of the past could help keep it contained. Almost as if it had never happened. I did not know of these books you speak of. That you or others not born in my time could know of what happened. That there would be a written record. I hadn't thought of the incident beyond my own experience." He looked at me. "Yes, Clara. I would like to tell you what happened. There is no reason any longer to keep it to myself. And if there is anyone I would speak it to, it would be you."

Tears welled in the corners of my eyes. I wasn't sure if it was because I was about to hear the real story of what happened with William. Or because he valued our friendship as much as I did.

William sat forward and adjusted his uniform jacket. "Yes, it's true. I was hanged."

There it was. Out in the open. "William, I'm so sorry."

"You have nothing to be sorry for."

I wanted to explain that was just an expression people said when there has been a death or an unfortunate event, but I knew now wasn't the time for a teachable moment.

William stood and walked toward the windows of the hotel room, where Boy was lying with his eyes closed on his bed beside his woolly mammoth. "That group of men and women we saw by the town hall ..."

"What about them?"

"The last time I saw a group of people congregating in that way, in that very place, was the day of my death."

My breathing became ragged, as if my throat was closing. William's death had been a public spectacle? How awful. *No, no, no.* This was all wrong. I should never have suggested that William talk about his past. There were too many painful memories. "I'm so sorry you had to see that, and please, if you don't want to, you don't—"

"I want to, Clara."

I nodded.

He stared out the window. "You haven't asked me why."

"Why what?"

"Why I was hanged."

"I ... I ..." The letters of the word *treason* blinked in my mind like a neon sign. "But, I don't ... it doesn't—"

"What did your research tell you?"

"Um ..." I shrugged. "Not very much. Only that, well, you drew your sword and killed a Union soldier. Some man named Nathan Newbury. Nothing else."

William nodded. "And you read this in a book?"

"Yes, at the library."

William took in the information. What could he be feeling? Not only had this terrible thing happened, but to find out that people all through history knew about it must be difficult. It was the 1800s version of someone leaking the personal aspects of your life on social media, which was basically a worldwide town square. And there was nothing you could do about it. People's interpretations—what others wrote about you—was usually what history tended to remember.

"Did you read anything else?" he asked. He was taking this far better than I thought a ghost should. Very even and thoughtful. No anger. There was never anger when it came to William. Well, only when he was protecting me from Joe.

I thought about the word I had been avoiding.

"You can tell me, Clara. It's all right."

I took a deep breath. "Well, one book said ... it said ..."

"Clara ..."

"It said that you were a ... *traitor*."

For the first time, I saw William wince. As if the word had stung him like a bee.

"William, for what it's worth," I said quickly, "I don't feel like this can be true. I know I didn't know you when you were ... well, alive, but I know you now. And the man I see before me could never be traitorous or harm anyone. You are kind and generous."

"I did slay him, Clara," William said softly. "I slayed Nathan Newbury."

"Well," I stood up from the bed, "if you did, then I am sure you had a very good reason."

He looked at me, intrigued. "How can you be certain?"

"Like I said, William. I never knew you, but I *know* you. I've developed a sense about people." I reached for the compass pendant around my neck and rubbed it. "And I know that ... well, your heart may no longer be beating, but it's a big one."

The side of William's mouth curved up a little. "You believe that?"

"Yes, I do."

"I'm not sure you believe there is a reason for murder."

I crossed my arms. "Maybe you were protecting yourself from this Nathan Newbury. That would be self-defense."

"If you believed self-defense was a reason for murder, you would have murdered your husband long ago."

I stood there, not knowing what to say. It always amazed me how perceptive William was. He had known me a short time, and yet seemed to know me so well. He was right. I could never bring myself to harm Joe, even after all the harm he had done to me.

"Violence is never the answer," William said. "I reckon you believe that, too." He glanced at Boy, who was emitting tiny snores. "Would you care to hear what happened?"

Yes! Yes! For the love of God, yes! "Well, only if you want to tell me," I said calmly, sitting back down.

William took another deep, air-less inhale. "When I joined the Union army, I knew nothing of battle. I was a shoe and boot maker here in Salem."

I remembered reading that. William as a nineteenth-century DSW Shoes? I couldn't help but smile. "I love that."

"Indeed. I learned the trade from my father, who learned it from his father before him. But when Confederate troops fired on Fort Sumter, I was eager to uphold the way of life we knew here in the North." He shook his head. "But I knew very little of war. I was very naïve. Nathan Newbury came from a prominent family in Salem. He was well-known and well-liked. But ... not by me."

"Why is that?"

"I had grown up with Nathan. Attended school together. Ran around, as kids do, in the wilderness together."

I could not picture reserved William Kensington running around in the woods.

"You get a sense of someone when you are in near proximity to them in ways others might not comprehend," William said. "I know you can understand that, Clara."

I thought again of Joe and nodded.

"Because of his family's wealth and influence, Nathan Newbury traveled greatly, and as we matured into adulthood, I came to see his beliefs had changed. Although perhaps they had always been that way. But they were very much in line with those who supported the Confederacy."

"How did you know this?"

"In small ways. When we attended Sunday mass, I would overhear him use biblical passages to justify slavery. 'Twas the power of one man over another that attracted him. Nathan Newbury may have been reared in the North, but his heart—if one can call it that—was in the southern way of life. After Fort Sumter, Nathan, like me and many others our age, enlisted in the Union army. But I knew, and I believe others knew as well, that his allegiance was to the South."

"Wait a second." I pushed myself forward on the bed. "Are you saying that Nathan Newbury was working against the war effort in the North? That he was a spy for the South?"

"He was not the only one, and I cannot say with certainty, but yes. There were signs. Once, I saw him conversing with another soldier, carrying a map that seemed to detail the Union supply routes. There would be no reason for a soldier of his rank to have that. Another time, he had in his possession documents written in code—some kind of secret communication. This is circumstantial, yes, but also suspicious. But then ...”

“Then what?” I was on the edge of my seat.

“One night, I was in the barracks alone and found a piece of paper lying under Nathan’s bed. I picked it up. ’Twas Confederate currency, which would be highly unusual for a Union soldier to carry. That was the third sign. I intended to inform my commanding officer. But that is when Nathan walked in and discovered me holding the Confederate bill.”

I gasped. “What happened?”

“He drew his saber upon me, and I was forced to draw mine as well. I’ve wondered for many years why he had drawn his saber. Perhaps he knew there was no talking to me about this. He knew I was a respectable man—just as I knew he was not. He came at me, and in the squabble, I struck a fatal blow.” William winced again. “As Nathan Newbury lay dying, he yelled for help and, as others arrived, accused me of treachery. He said it was *he* who had discovered the Confederate money and maps on *my* bed, and that I had killed him because of it.”

“But that wasn’t true!”

“The truth has no place in war, Clara.”

“What happened next?”

“As I said, there were others working with Nathan. Some of them were soldiers of influence, and they knew the dangers I posed. These co-conspirators banded together, worried that I would divulge they, too, were acting as spies. They perpetuated Nathan's lies and told my commanding officer I had attacked Nathan for having discovered my plot, and that it was *I* who was the spy."

"No! What did you do?"

"I denied it, of course, but the evidence was overwhelming." He looked at me. "It was my word against theirs."

"And they hanged you for that?"

He nodded. "Not long after. There was a trial of sorts, but by then they had made up their minds. Someone needed to pay. My lone voice of innocence was not to be heard among the masses. I was hanged along with several common criminals."

I wanted to hug him. I wanted to run to William and wrap my arms around him (if I could even do that), but I didn't know how he would react. He was already uncomfortable being in this bedroom with me. I needed to respect his boundaries. I simply leaned back against the headboard. "William, that is terrible. I am so sorry."

"It is what it is."

"So, you weren't besties with John Wilkes Booth?"

William furrowed his brow. "Booth? The actor?"

"Well, yes, but he's also the one who assassinated President Abraham Lincoln."

William's pale blue eyes opened wide. He sat back down in the chair. "I had not heard. In what year?"

"Eighteen sixty-five. Not even a week after the Civil War ended."

William appeared winded. If that were possible. He didn't speak for some time and then said, "I voted for Mister Lincoln in the eighteen-sixty election. He was a good man. I met him once when I was a young man."

"You met Abraham Lincoln?!"

He nodded. "I shook hands with him briefly. He was campaigning for Zachary Taylor, the Whig candidate in the eighteen-forty-eight presidential election. He had very kind eyes. Why did you believe I was on friendly terms with John Wilkes Booth?"

I got up and showed him the photo on my phone. "This photo of the two of you appeared in a library book."

William studied the image. "I had gone to see a play featuring Mr. Booth. Afterward, he spoke with theatergoers. A local newspaper photographer took that image. I recall posing for it."

Could this really all be a mistake? A misunderstanding? I was feeling relieved. "And here I thought the two of you were having secret meetings in the basement of Kensington House." I laughed, but William wasn't laughing.

Why wasn't he laughing?

"I did have surreptitious meetings in the lower areas of Kensington House, as you call it," he said plainly.

"Wait, you did? Did those meetings have anything to do with the trapdoor I saw down there?"

"Yes."

My mind was reeling. "Wait, were you doing things that were illegal?"

"In some parts of the country, yes."

I searched his face for understanding. What exactly was William telling me?

He must have sensed my confusion. "Are you familiar with the term Underground Railroad?" he asked.

"The Underground Railroad???" I had to sit down again. "Are you telling me you were helping escaped slaves, that Kensington House was a stop on the Underground Railroad?"

He nodded. "That trapdoor, as you called it, was often used to shuttle people from safe harbor to safe harbor. There are more than a few trapdoors throughout Salem."

I didn't know what to say. Ask him if he knew Harriet Tubman? Ask him if he was scared the underground network would be discovered? I just sat there and let William continue.

"I sometimes helped fashion the men, women, and children—there were children—new shoes during their stay at Kensington House. Many had soles that were worn clear through. The rooms on the upstairs level—"

"The secret rooms?"

"Yes, some stayed there temporarily. Others stayed in the basement until we could find another safe place. I was well aware that Confederate sympathizers like Nathan Newbury would be very dangerous to our cause, so we had to be careful."

"Is that why there are numbers and letters written on the walls in the basement? It has to do with the Underground Railroad?"

"Correct. Some of the former slaves wanted to practice their writing. Or learn to read and write. I would etch numbers and letters on the wall as a visual aid."

I found myself hyperventilating. With so much pent-up excitement—and anger. William Kensington was a hero. And the world believed him to be a traitor. "We have to tell somebody!"

"Clara—"

"You are innocent of everything I've read in every book."

"I am guilty, Clara."

"I know we both don't believe in violence, but you killed Nathan Newbury, a traitor, as you were defending yourself from imminent danger. That is self-defense under the law, whether or not we morally agree with it. It was his life or yours."

"It turned out to be both of our lives," William said sadly. "No matter the reason, I brought humiliation and dishonor to my regiment, which will be known henceforth as the regiment of a traitor."

"That may be so, but, William, history believes *you* are the traitor. The traitor was Nathan Newbury. We need to right the record."

"What does it matter, Clara? I have come to terms with what I have done."

"It matters to me and would matter to a lot of people. And I think it matters to you, too. When I first met you, you told me you believed you caused all the misery in your family due to your actions. You did not. You acted honorably, and the world deserves to know that. Nathan Newbury doesn't get to be a hero."

"Bad people often do, Clara."

"Well, not if we can help it."

"We?"

I stood up again and bent down in front of William. "I know you have fight in you. I saw the way you stood up to Joe, how you helped me. Fighting doesn't have to mean violence. You are proof of that. Fighting means advocacy. Together, I think we make a great team, and—"

Buzz.

Was that my phone? Who could be calling me at this hour? I hurried to the table and looked at the phone screen.

Buzz.

"Are you going to see who is contacting you through your pocket device?" William asked.

"I don't know who it is. I don't recognize the phone number."

"The courteous thing to do is answer and discover who the caller is."

Clearly, he was not familiar with telemarketers.

Against my better judgment, I swiped. "Hello?"

"Hi, Clara?"

"Yes."

"This is Penelope Givens."

"Oh, Penelope, hi. Are you all right?"

There was a pause, and then Penelope said, "I think for the first time in a long time, I *am* all right. Because of you, Clara. I want to thank you for what you've done. For giving me back this manuscript. I had felt so lost for so long. The enormity of having this back in my possession hit me after you left. You didn't have to bring this here. You went out of your way to do that, and I greatly appreciate it."

"It was my pleasure." I looked at William and smiled. With any luck, I'd be able to right William's wrong, too.

"A big part of me had lost hope, thinking no one was going to believe I wrote a best-selling book, but now I think it's worth a try."

"What are you going to do?"

"I reached out to my old landlord. We had been friendly before my mom and I moved out. He was a decent man. I took a chance and asked him if he had any of my old mail, and he said he did! He had been holding it for me. He thought one day he might see me again. I asked if there was a package, and he said yes, in a yellow envelope. Clara, I think that's the manuscript I mailed to myself. If it is, that would be proof that I wrote *The Secrets We Keep*."

"That's amazing, Penelope!"

"My mom has always told me, if we don't fight for ourselves, no one will."

I looked at William again. "I agree. That's good advice."

"I know this is a lot to ask, but do you think you can come over tomorrow to our place in Swampscott? I'm just so excited, and I don't know where to start. Maybe we can figure it out together? Or I can meet you somewhere else."

"I'd be happy to come over."

"Thank you!" Penelope said. "I've already filled out the discharge paperwork, and I'm set to meet with my doctor in the morning. If all goes well, I will be home by afternoon with the package in my hand. My mother is so excited. She wants to cook. Do you like quiche?"

"I love quiche."

"Great, so I'll meet you there?"

"Of course. I already know the address."

"I don't want to look back anymore, Clara. I want to look forward. See you tomorrow."

"I'll see you then," I said and ended the call.

"Who might that be?" William asked.

"That was Penelope Givens."

"Is she your friend?"

I smiled. "Maybe one day. But right now, she is someone who is restarting her life again after a terrible fall. I'm going to help her."

"You seem to make a habit of doing that."

"And I say we do the same for you."

William shook his head. "It is too late for me, Clara. I appreciate the desire."

"It's never too late." I grabbed my yoga pants and changed in the bathroom. When I came out, Boy was off his little bed and putting his paws on the side of my bed. I picked him up, placed him on the blanket, and crawled next to him.

"Do you really believe that?" William asked. "That it is never too late?"

"Yes," I said as Boy spun in circles and plopped down beside me. I pulled the covers over us. "Good night, William." I turned over and rested my hand on Boy's black-and-white spotted belly. Tomorrow was going to be a new day. For Penelope. For William. I closed my eyes.

"Excuse me, Clara?"

"Yes?" I opened my eyes.

"Regarding our conversation earlier, you should know that Kensington House is not my house."

I sat up. "It isn't?"

"No." He pulled down on the gray shirt sleeves of his army jacket. "It is your house, too. It is *ours*."

I smiled and put my head back on the pillow.

Tomorrow was going to be a new day for me, too.

Chapter 26

THE NEXT MORNING WHEN I awoke, Boy was sleeping next to me, but William was gone.

"William?" I called as Boy let out a big yawn and bent down into a downward dog-type yoga pose.

I got out of bed and checked the bathroom, which was empty. Not that I expected William to be in there. "Where did he go?" I said to Boy.

Bark!

I looked at the table and saw a note written on the hotel stationery in William's neat penmanship.

Clara,

I returned to Kensington House to supervise the electrician. He appears to misplace his telephone device often. I have to keep returning it to his work area. Let us hope he does better with the

wires. The plumber should be returning this afternoon.
With any luck, he will wear a belt this time.
Signed,
William

I smiled and looked at Boy. "William's on top of things over there."

Bark!

"Okay, buddy, we're going to do a quick walk and a quick meal, and then you're going to hang out here for a while with Woolly Mammoth and your other toys while I run a few errands. The house is too dangerous for you to stay there. Okay?"

Bark!

"All right, let's get started."

I HURRIED TOWARD YE Olde Salem Book Shoppe. My first order of business: find Marlena. There was much to tell her. Especially that I was off the case, and the Salem Police Department was going to take it from here. She would have to understand. I had done as much as I could, but how was I supposed to find a blond woman with a tattoo? I just didn't have the resources.

The skies were cloudy, but the onset of summer was bringing tourists into Salem, so the streets were more crowded than usual. I could only imagine how it would be during Halloween season. I might have to get Boy a stroller, so he wouldn't get stepped on!

Ronnie was standing outside Haute Chocolate with Sissy, the owner, and they were pointing at the front windows of the store. Probably redecorating. When Ronnie saw me and waved, and then Sissy did the same, a warm feeling went through me. I was becoming part of the fabric of Salem. People were recognizing me. Getting to know me. My neighbors had never really gotten the chance on Long Island. Joe was always shadowing me. Watching my every move. Now people would get to know the *real* me.

As I passed The Haunted Cookie, Alice was placing samples outside. I waved to her, thinking my good luck with Ronnie and Sissy would continue, but she only glanced at me and didn't wave back. That Alice was a tough nut to crack. She was clearly interested in Marlena's book since she had been to the book signing, and she showed up at the writers' workshop. Did that mean she had an interest in writing, too? There seemed to be so much under the surface with Alice. Beckett, while we were solving his murder, once mentioned Alice had an anger management problem, but I hadn't seen any of that. She seemed so quiet and reserved.

As I continued walking, I thought of all the suggestions I could make to guests of my soon-to-be bed-and-breakfast.

You must check out The Haunted Cookie. They have the best donuts. I especially love the Fluffernutter. Wait, do you like chocolate? You've GOT to go to Haute Chocolate. The thought of making people's vacations the best they could be filled me with joy. This was what I had gone to school for. This was what I was always supposed to do. It took more than eight years to get back on track, but it was nice to know that Joe hadn't derailed my career entirely. And, hopefully, one day *I* would be the one doing the traveling. That had always been the plan.

Ye Olde Salem Book Shoppe had just opened, and there were quite a few people outside. More of the Marlena Ryder effect, I was sure. I didn't see her anywhere, so I went inside the bookstore, hoping she was roaming around. If she wasn't, I wasn't sure where else to go. Other than the library.

"Hey, how's it going?" Aaron was standing by the register, placing labels on books.

"Hi, Aaron. Thanks for the books."

"No problem." He wiped his brow. "Still busy. And we just opened. People seem to be coming just because of … you know, what happened with Marlena." He shook his head. "Business is good, but you feel kind of guilty, you know."

"I totally get it. But think of it this way. It just shows how much people loved Marlena and her writing. They still want to be a part of her world."

"That's a good way to look at it. And here I was think-ing people were just morbid." He laughed. "Here for more books about Salem?"

Actually, I'm here looking for Marlena's ghost. "Nah, just browsing."

"Well, if you need anything, let me know."

I drifted toward the Marlena Ryder display that featured the cardboard cutout of her, which had been moved to an-other section near the back of the store. Sadie was there, talking to ... ugh, Taylor from the *Salem Chronicle. They must be talking about the murder.* As much as I would have rather not dealt with Taylor, I was curious to hear if there had been any updates. I nonchalantly walked over and pretended to browse the bookstore's memoir section.

"As I told you, Taylor, I just found her there," Sadie said. "It was awful. I can't seem to get the image out of my head."

"You don't remember seeing anyone come through here?"

"No, but I was busy. A little girl needed my help at the front of the store."

"And there's no other way in?" Taylor asked.

Sadie shook her head. "No. Other than, you know, the trapdoor."

Ah, the trap door!

"But like many houses in Salem, we boarded that up. It only accesses a tiny crawl space, which is where we used to keep toiletries and plumbing supplies. Whoever did this had to come through this door." She pointed.

Well, that solved that. The murderer was looking more and more like the blond woman with the tattoo.

"And there are no security cameras here?" Taylor asked, pointing around the bathroom door.

Sadie shook her head. "We only have them at the front of the store and at the register. Never in my wildest dreams did I ever think I'd need a security camera in front of the bathroom." She suddenly looked at me. "Hi, nice to see you again. Can I help you with anything?"

"No, I'm just browsing," I said as Taylor glanced at me and then did a double take. Before he could make a sarcastic remark, I turned and was about to walk away when I saw Marlena standing in front of me.

"Do you see where they put me?" she asked, pointing to the cardboard cutout of herself. "It's only been a few days, and I've been relegated to the back of the store already."

I put in my earbuds and walked toward the display—and away from Taylor. "Maybe it's like the supermarket."

"The supermarket?"

"Yeah, like, they put popular items—milk, eggs—at the back of the store so that shoppers will have to go through the entire store to get to them. And along the way, they tend to pick up other items. It's a way to get people to buy more. Maybe Sadie is doing the same thing."

"So it's not a demotion, but a promotion?"

"Exactly."

The idea seemed to perk up Marlena a little. "Where have you been?" she asked. "How did it go with ... you know, Penelope?"

"That's why I'm here. I have a lot to tell you."

"You do? What is it?"

"C'mon, I'll tell you on the way."

"On the way where?"

"You'll see. And, this time, we're driving."

Chapter 27

"I really don't want to do this," Marlena said as we walked into the building where Penelope lived with her mother.

I knew she didn't, but I wasn't taking no for an answer. Marlena needed to see Penelope, see the happiness in her eyes for having her manuscript back. I wanted Marlena to realize what she had taken from Penelope by claiming the novel was hers, to see the damage she had done. And how good it felt to help undo some of that damage. "I think it's important."

"But what about my murder?" she asked.

"As I told you in the car, the Salem Police Department is on your case."

"There's no guarantee that blond woman with the tattoo murdered me."

"It's a solid lead, Marlena."

"Thanks to you. Based on what you told me, the detectives wouldn't have known the woman with the tattoo was suspicious until you pointed out that she was leaving the bookstore with fewer books than she purchased. How can I rely on *them* to find my killer? I need *you*."

"Marlena, they're professionals. That was just a lucky break on my part."

"You have skills, Clara. You're good at this. When are you going to—"

"*Shhhh ...*" I said as we approached a woman at the front desk.

"Why are you shushing me?" Marlena asked. "She can't hear me."

I knew she couldn't, but I didn't want to talk about Marlena's case anymore. I wanted to move on. Marlena was in capable hands. I knew that, but then why was I feeling so guilty?

"Can I help you?" asked the woman at the front desk. She was young and perky, probably just out of college, and reminded me of me when I had first started out in hospitality. Hopefully, her career trajectory would be better than mine.

"I'm here to see Mrs. Givens," I said. It felt good not having to slip in undetected this time.

"And your name is?"

"Clara. Clara Kelly."

The young woman checked her computer screen and smiled. "Yes, Ms. Kelly, you're expected." She pointed to the elevators. "Right that way. Eighth floor. I'll let her know you're on your way."

As I got on the elevator with Marlena and the door closed, she said, "This isn't the last of this discussion, you know."

"What discussion?"

"About you finding my killer. You're a nice person, Clara. I've gotten to know you. I wish I had gotten to know you when I was ... well, alive. I trust you. I don't trust anybody else."

This didn't surprise me. Marlena had stolen another author's book from her and claimed it as her own. Joe had stolen quite a few things, too, when he was alive—alcohol, cash, the neighbor's lawn mower—and he didn't trust anyone, either. The most untrustworthy of people tended to be the ones who trusted the least.

Before I could respond, the elevator dinged and the doors slid apart. By the time we reached Penelope's apartment door, it opened, and Penelope's mother ran toward me and wrapped me in a giant bear hug.

"You saved my daughter!" she exclaimed. "My Penny ... she's back. And she sounds like she used to. Hopeful. Ambitious. You put the light back into her."

"I don't think that light ever left, Mrs. Givens," I said as she released me. "It just got dimmed for a little bit."

"Well, my Penny told me what you did, how you gave her back the book that awful woman stole from her!"

I glanced at Marlena, whose eyes found the floor.

"Please, please come in," Penelope's mother said.

As Marlena and I walked inside, I said, "Something smells delicious."

"It's Penelope's favorite. Quiche. I'm so glad you'll be able to join us for lunch." She ran her hands along her bare arms. "Is it a bit chilly in here?"

"No, it's fine," I said, although I had been around ghosts more than most people and had gotten used to the cold.

"She's not home yet." Penelope's mom closed a window. "She's running a little late. Please make yourself at home."

I couldn't believe the change in Penelope's mother since the last time Marlena and I had visited. She was so much friendlier. And happier. Probably because there was some closure regarding her daughter. I didn't remember much about my mother, but I recalled her telling me that a mother was only as happy as her least-happy child. I may have been only eight years old when my mother died of uterine cancer, but I remembered how blue she could be when I fell and scraped my knee. It was like she, herself, had gotten bruised. Penelope's happiness had become her mother's happiness. "You have a lovely home," I said, motioning toward the large living room and its warm, beige-y tones.

"Thank you. It's not really mine," Penelope's mother said. "We're staying here until we find our own place."

"Well, it's still home, even if it's just temporary. And it's lovely." I remembered how much I thought of Kensington

House as home even though I had originally planned to stay there for a short time.

"That's kind of you to say. Would you like something to drink? And please call me Yolanda."

"Thank you, Yolanda. Water is fine."

"You look so familiar to me. I thought so the last time you stopped by, too."

"You know, you're right. You look a bit familiar as well."

"And your hair!" Yolanda reached out and touched the bottom of my red tresses. "It's so lovely. I don't see very many redheads as clients."

"Cleaning clients?"

"No," she said with a laugh, "I'm sort of a Jaclyn of all trades. In addition to running my own cleaning service, I also cut hair."

"That must be where Penelope gets her entrepreneurial spirit from."

"I guess." Yolanda shrugged. "When you don't have a lot of money growing up, you learn quickly that you need to do anything you can to stay afloat. Life can be unfair, and sometimes you need to level the playing field. Now, let me get you that water."

As she headed toward the kitchen, I looked for Marlena, who was walking around the room.

"Nice place," Marlena said. "What did she mean, the place isn't hers?"

"Penelope mentioned that she and her mother are staying here while the tenants are overseas," I whispered. "Yolanda is such a valued worker that the apartment owners don't want to lose her, so they're letting her stay here until she finds a new place. Isn't that wonderful? To be valued so much?"

"Indeed, it is." Marlena was looking out the balcony doors, which overlooked the complex's pool. Some diehards were out there swimming even though the weather wasn't quite so warm. "What's in here?" she asked, turning her attention to a tiny hallway that led to three more doorways.

It shouldn't have surprised me that Marlena was so nosy.

One doorway led to a bedroom, another to a bathroom, and the last looked like it opened into a bedroom that also functioned as a workroom or office. A little chair was set up with a cape over it. There were blow dryers, scissors, combs, and towels lying about.

"This is where the magic happens," Yolanda said with a laugh as she handed me my glass of water.

"It's a nice set-up," I said.

"Yeah, I have a client coming this afternoon for a highlight." She looked at my hair. "You know ... while we're waiting for Penelope, I can give you a trim, if you like."

"A trim?"

"Sorry. Occupational hazard. I can't help but notice when it's been a while since someone's last haircut." Yolanda shrugged. "I can spot a dead end a mile away."

"Oh," I said, touching my hair and now completely self-conscious about my dead ends. No wonder I had been so lax with Boy's haircuts; I hardly took care of my own. "No, that's all right."

"You *could* use a trim, if you ask me," Marlena said with a roll of her eyes.

"I insist. On the house," Yolanda said. "For everything you've done for my Penny. I won't take no for an answer." Yolanda took the cape off the chair.

Marlena indicated with her eyes that if I didn't take advantage of a free haircut, then there must be something wrong with me. I placed my water on a nearby table, sat down in the chair, and Yolanda snapped the cape around my neck.

"Great!" Yolanda said.

As she dampened my hair with a spray bottle, I glanced around the room at all the hair care products—mousse, conditioner, detangling combs. They reminded me of my mom, who was a bit of a powder puff and always said that if she hadn't worked in a bank, she would have been a hairstylist. I could still see myself sitting at her vanity as a little girl and pretending to curl my hair with the unplugged curling iron. She loved putting my hair in all sorts of different styles—braids, ponytails, headbands. "You need to show off this beautiful red hair," she would often say, never knowing that, one day, I would have to cover it all up with a blond wig to escape a bad marriage.

At the far end of the room was a table with several Styrofoam mannequin heads sporting wigs. "Do you make wigs as well?"

"Ah, no, those are for clients who are losing their hair for whatever reason. Maybe they're going through chemotherapy or have alopecia. We work together to come up with a style that suits them."

"Do you have a lot of hair clients?"

"Quite a few longtime clients." Yolanda combed the back of my damp hair. "How much do you want off the back?"

"Maybe about an inch?"

Yolanda nodded and began to cut. "So, do you have a big family, Clara?"

"No, not really. It's just me."

"Just you?"

"Yeah, both my parents died. And ... well, so did my husband."

"I'm so sorry. No sisters or brothers?"

"Nope, but I have a good friend," I said, thinking of William as my eyes continued roaming around the room.

On the wall were lines of photographs showing women with different hairstyles. Most of the photos were of wedding parties, all the girls laughing and posing coquettishly. One was of a mother and daughter with matching haircuts.

"These photos are beautiful," I said.

"Thank you. I work hard at what I do."

I glanced at Marlena, who was standing by the lighted mirror, leaning back against it. "She does good work," she said.

I looked again at the photo of the mother and daughter. Something about it was drawing my attention. I wasn't sure what it was. "Who is that photo of there?" I asked, pointing.

Yolanda ran her hand through my hair. "I think you're done," she said and then looked up at the photo I indicated. "Oh, that was a wedding I did about six months ago. In Connecticut."

Connecticut? No, that wasn't it. I had never been to Connecticut. (Unless you counted traveling through it.) Still, something was bothering me—a hum in my brain, like an electric current. "What are their names? The two women?"

"Why, do you know them?" Yolanda asked. "A beautiful family. The bride's name is Nikki. Last name was Ryan, I think. Her mom is Sylvia."

Nikki Ryan and Sylvia Ryan. The names didn't ring any bells. *What was bothering me about that photo?*

"It was a beautiful affair." Yolanda brushed the hair off my cape. "I did the hair for the entire bridal party and the mother of the bride. And look ..." She pointed at the women's hands. "I also did the temporary tattoos for the bridal party. That's a thing now, apparently. It's great because I'm able to upsell. I've been a tattoo artist for years. I can do permanent or temporary, for those who don't want to take the plunge. They can last anywhere from two to six days. It's good money. Like I said, anything that helps put bread on the table, right?"

A jolt of electricity shot through me. I gripped onto the arms of the chair I was sitting in to steady myself.

"What's the matter?" Marlena and Yolanda asked me simultaneously.

"You don't look too good," Yolanda said. "Do you want your water?"

"Are you okay?" Marlena prodded.

I was *not* okay. The tattoos. *That* was what was bothering me. On the mother's and daughter's hands. That geometric design. That was the same tattoo the blond woman had at Sadie's bookshop the day of Marlena's murder. Were those women involved somehow?

Wait ... *Blond woman.*

Right below the photo of the bride and her mother was a Styrofoam mannequin head—with a blond wig.

A wig ...

Detective Daniels was looking for a blond woman with a tattoo. What if the person who had killed Marlena was not a blond woman with a tattoo but a brunette who had been wearing a blond wig and had been sporting a temporary tattoo? Why hadn't I thought of that before? After all, I was no stranger to blond wigs.

I looked at Yolanda, who was peering at me curiously, the scissors still in her hand. Had she worn that wig to the book signing and given herself a temporary tattoo as a disguise?

She certainly had motive. And the more I scrutinized her face—blocking out the dark hair—I realized I *had* seen her before. Sitting right next to me at the book signing.

What should I do?

Tiptoe out of here quietly? Come up with some excuse? Would Yolanda hurt me if she knew what I knew if what I knew was true?

"What's going on with you, Clara?" Marlena asked.

Yolanda, though, was quiet. Her eyes were boring into mine—searching. Then her face changed from focused to confused to ... *angry*. She looked again like the woman Marlena and I had seen when we first visited her apartment.

"It was you," I blurted. "Wasn't it?"

"What was who?" Marlena asked, confused. "What are you talking about, Clara?"

"You ..." Yolanda tightened her grip on the scissors in her hand. "I knew I recognized you. You were at the book signing."

"*You* were at the book signing?" Marlena asked Yolanda with surprise.

I wondered what would come next. Would Yolanda explain? Sit me down to a quiche lunch and calmly tell me what happened? But then I saw it. A little gleam in Yolanda's narrowing eyes. That little tell. The same tell Joe used to get right before he was about to pounce.

There was no time to waste. I quickly stood, grabbed the knob of the door to the room, and ran out, pulling the door shut as Yolanda lurched toward me.

"Open this door at once!" Yolanda was shouting. "There's nothing to be afraid of!"

That was a lie. I didn't need to see her face to know that. I pulled on the doorknob with all my weight to keep the door closed as Yolanda yanked from the other side.

"You don't understand what it's like!" Yolanda shouted. "To watch someone become rich and famous when they never had any right to be!"

She was shouting something else, but it was difficult to understand because Marlena realized what was happening and was yelling over her.

"You stole my life from me!" Marlena was screaming.

"Marlena, she can't hear you!" I cried. "You have to concentrate. I need you to come in here and get me my phone while I hold the door closed. I need to call the police."

"Let me out, and I'll get your phone for you!" Yolanda said, pulling hard on the door, which opened a bit, but I used my body weight to snap it closed.

"Why can't she feel me?!" Marlena was shouting. "I'm trying to hit her!"

"It takes practice! You need to focus!" Wait, I think *I* needed to focus. "Marlena, you have to look at the big picture. We need to call the police *now*!"

"I'm not Marlena!" Yolanda was shouting. "Marlena is dead!"

"Yeah, because of you!" Marlena shrieked.

"Marlena, listen to me!" I yelled.

"My name is Yolanda! Open the door! I'll write it down for you!"

"Marlena," I called, "can you walk through this wall?!"

"Walk through the wall???!" Yolanda yelled.

"Walk through the wall???!" Marlena echoed. "I don't know! I'm afraid to try! I can *lean* on the wall!"

Okay, *leaning* wasn't going to help me.

Just then, the doorknob broke apart, and I fell back into the living room as the door to Yolanda's office/bedroom swung open. I quickly stood as Yolanda entered the living room, still carrying the scissors. Was that the weapon she had used to kill Marlena? Was the *murder* weapon in her hands?

I put my hands in front of me as Yolanda and I began circling the living room like wrestlers. I practically looked like one, since I was still wearing the hair-cutting cape around me. *Stone Cold Clara Kelly.* Outside, near the pool, someone was yelling *Marco!*, followed by *Polo!*.

"Marlena, get my phone," I said calmly when Marlena entered the room.

"Clara, she killed me," Marlena said, a sob sounding like it was stuck in her throat. "You need to be careful. I know what she's capable of."

"I know, and that's why you need to get my phone," I said.

"I don't know why you keep calling me Marlena," Yolanda said, watching me closely, "but I'm afraid I'm not going to get your phone for you since you came in here and tried to kill me."

"Um, what are you talking about?" I asked as my eyes searched for my purse. There it was. On the coffee table. My phone was only a few feet away, stuffed inside.

"Self-defense, right?" Yolanda was saying. "I won't go to jail if I have to kill you in self-defense."

My mind turned to William. How he had killed Nathan Newbury in self-defense. That was the story he had told me. And I believed him. Wholeheartedly. Would anybody believe Yolanda?

"Is that why you killed Marlena Ryder?" I asked. "Was it self-defense, too?"

"Let's call it self-*preservation*," Yolanda said with a smile. "You hurt me or my baby, and I'll come at you with everything I have. What was it you called me? *Entrepreneurial*, right, Clara?"

That was before I knew you were a cold-blooded killer, I thought as, suddenly, Yolanda charged toward me with the scissors. Just as I expected to feel the sharp point sink into my chest, she lurched to the side and fell backward, shrieking, "How are you doing that?"

With Yolanda on the floor, I reached for my purse on the coffee table, but it was gone. *What?!* Then I saw it. In the air.

Marlena was holding it, but to Yolanda, it must have looked like it was floating on its own.

"Marlena," I said, "you got it!"

"Don't talk to me. I'm concentrating," she said, but then the purse fell to the floor. "You distracted me!"

The purse fell between Yolanda and me, and we both lunged for it. I got to it first, and Yolanda grabbed my arm, and I was afraid she was going to stab me when a voice cut through the commotion.

"What is going on here?!"

Penelope.

She was standing in the doorway of the apartment, holding a manila envelope in her hands. I froze as I wondered if Penelope was in on the whole thing, if I had misjudged her character, if she had led me here so that she could do away with me, but then Yolanda pulled away from me—as if embarrassed—and stood. Before Yolanda could say anything, I quickly said, "Penelope, your mother killed Marlena Ryder."

"What?!" Penelope asked, and I could tell her surprise was genuine.

She didn't know.

"Mom, what is she talking about?" Penelope asked Yolanda.

"Wait, Penny, let me explain," Yolanda said.

I quickly grabbed my purse from the floor and dug around for my phone to call 9-1-1 when Yolanda broke into tears.

"Penny, that woman destroyed you," Yolanda said. "She broke your spirit. I felt so helpless, watching her get all that acclaim, all that attention. Meanwhile, my bright light of a little girl was leaving me, falling into a depression. I was so angry."

"Momma ..."

"I don't know what came over me. I saw that she was having a book signing, and I just thought if she was gone, then maybe there was a chance that you would get the recognition you deserve. She was a thief, Penny. She was a very bad person."

"That may be so, Momma, but she didn't deserve to die." Penny began to cry.

This poor woman. Having her book stolen from her. An extended stay in a psychiatric hospital, only to discharge herself and find out her mother was a murderer.

Finally, I found my phone. *Why was my purse such a black hole?* I was about to turn it on, but the battery was at 1 percent. *Noooooo!* I had forgotten to charge it last night. William's Nathan Newbury story had gotten me off my routine. I tried to eke out a quick emergency call when the screen went dead.

Now what?

"We don't have to tell anybody." Yolanda was pointing at me. "We can say she came in to harm me. That she had gone to visit you yesterday at the hospital and blamed me for putting you there. Penny, we can do away with her. She said she has no family. No one who cares about her. She's *alone*."

"She's *not* alone," Marlena said, standing between Yolanda and me. "She has *me*. Clara Kelly is just about the most decent person I've ever met. And I'm proud to call myself her friend."

I was trying to figure out another plan. Whether I could slide open the patio doors and leap into the community pool when Penny took out her phone.

"That's it, Pen," Yolanda said. "I'll say I killed her when she came at me. When—"

"Hello," Penny said into her phone. "I'd like to report a murder."

"It's not murder, Pen," Yolanda whispered. "It'll be self-defense."

"Yes," Penelope said into the phone. "I think my mother killed best-selling author Marlena Ryder."

Chapter 28

"Penelope, what have you done?" Yolanda said, crumpling to the floor.

"No, Momma, it's what have *you* done." Penelope ended the call and turned her eyes toward me. "Go, Clara," she said sadly. "There's no need for you to get involved in this. You should leave."

I stood up next to Marlena. Penelope clearly had no idea how much I was *already* involved in this. I grabbed my purse, which contained my useless phone, and quickly headed toward the door of the apartment, but Marlena lingered.

"C'mon, Marlena," I whispered.

"For the love of God!" Yolanda shouted from the floor. "My name is Yolanda!"

Marlena started walking toward me but stopped when she got to Penelope.

"For what it's worth, I'm sorry," Marlena said to Penelope, who was looking down at her mother. "Turns out, you're not only a better writer than I'll ever be, but also a better person."

As Marlena and I got to the door, Penelope said, "Clara?"

"Yes?"

She held up the manila envelope in her hand. "I had been so excited to tell you when I got home. I was able to retrieve my manuscript from my old landlord. Look. The envelope is unopened. I have at least some proof that *The Secrets We Keep* is my book." She shook her head sadly. "This was going to be a fresh start."

"Maybe it still can be," I said as Yolanda began sobbing. "For both of you."

I walked into the hallway and stepped into the elevator with Marlena. The doors closed.

"I can't believe we did it," Marlena said as I pressed the Lobby button.

I couldn't believe it, either. "I know."

"I thought I would feel different."

"How do you feel?"

"I don't know. Stunned, I guess. I thought I would feel relieved. Triumphant, even. But I just feel shellshocked. And sad." She shrugged. "And I feel responsible. I know it was a terrible thing that Yolanda did, but I also know it was a terrible thing that *I* did. To Penelope. It's not the same, I know. But, still, it wasn't right."

As we stepped out of the lobby and into the parking lot, sirens filled the air. Two police cars skidded to a stop in front of the building, and several police officers ran toward the entrance.

"What do you think will happen to Yolanda now?" Marlena asked.

"I don't know. I feel like I kind of understand Yolanda. I know what it's like to be so angry at someone, to want them ... well, dead. But we can't let bad people change who we are on the inside. If we do that, we never win."

Marlena smiled. "I meant what I said about you up there. I hope that we're friends."

"I think we are."

"Thank you, Clara. For everything." She looked up at the cloudy sky. "I think I feel it now."

"Feel what?"

"A kind of peace. You know, the kind like *rest in peace*. It's time for me to go."

"How do you know?"

"I don't know." She shrugged. "I just know. Goodbye, Clara Kelly."

"Goodbye, Marlena Ryder," I said as she smiled at me one last time and vanished.

WHEN I PULLED INTO the narrow driveway of Kensington House, I was surprised to see Sebastian sitting at my front door with a bouquet of flowers.

"Sebastian, hi, what are you doing here?"

"These are for you." He handed me the bouquet.

"But why?"

"Well, the last time we saw one another, you seemed upset. I wasn't sure why. I couldn't bear the thought that I had done something to upset you. But if I did, I thought I could do something to make it up to you."

"Was I upset?" I thought back to when I had last been at The Pampered Pup, which seemed like years ago. *Oh, that's right.* It was right after I had had an argument with Marlena. "Sebastian, it had nothing to do with you. I'm so sorry if you thought it did. I just had a lot on my mind that day."

"Are things better now?"

"Yes, much better." I smiled. "I think everything has been resolved."

"Good." Sebastian took a step closer to me.

Oh no.

"Clara, I have something to ask you."

Don't. Please.

"Tell me if I'm wrong, but ..."

He cleared his throat. He was nervous, which made me like him even more. How unsure he was. Joe had never been unsure. I used to find confidence attractive. Not so much anymore.

"I'm not sure if you know this about me," Sebastian said. "I'm kind of old-fashioned. I don't do the online dating thing. It just never felt right to me. I always thought it was best to get to know someone offline first. To see how they smile when I tell a really bad joke. Or to see what draws someone's eyes." He shuffled his feet. "Well, here goes, I was wondering if you'd like to have dinner sometime."

I wanted to say yes. I really did. "Sebastian ..."

"You can tell me if you're not interested. It's okay."

"It's not that. Really. It's just ..." I needed to tell him. Maybe by talking more about what had happened to me with Joe, I could finally free myself. And maybe the bad dreams would end. "I was in a very toxic relationship. For a long time. I was married for eight years."

"You were?" he asked, surprised.

I nodded. "It was just awful."

"I'm so sorry. Was he unkind?"

"More than unkind." I left it at that and hoped Sebastian didn't ask me anything more. He didn't. He let me continue.

"I'm just learning about myself for the first time. Maybe it's because I'm alone for the first time. My dad died earlier this year." I reached up and rubbed the compass pendant hanging around my neck.

"I'm so sorry."

"Thank you. It happened around the time I first came to Salem. Your offer is wonderful—*you're* wonderful—but I think I just want to become *me* before I become a *we*. Does that make any sense?"

Sebastian nodded. "It definitely does."

"Thank you for understanding." I tried to hand back the flowers.

"Please, keep them. As a gift." He smiled. "I'm here if you ever need anything."

"I appreciate that."

He turned to leave but stopped. "And who knows ... maybe one day, you know, in the future, if it's all right with you, I can ask you to dinner again. When you're feeling ... more like yourself."

"Definitely," I said with a smile. "I'd like that."

And as I watched Sebastian walk out of my driveway, I knew I meant it.

Chapter 29

"THANK YOU FOR EVERYTHING!" I called to the electrician, who waved as he backed out of my driveway.

Could it be?

For weeks, the electrician's and plumber's workers traipsed in and out of Kensington House—making a racket, making a mess. Finally, they were gone. I couldn't wait to enjoy the stillness, but before I could close the front door, I heard someone say, "Hey, Clara!"

Sebastian was walking into the driveway.

"Sebastian, hi! What are you doing here?"

He lifted his little briefcase. "I was just making a quick house call—I don't normally do that, but it's for a longtime customer who isn't feeling well. And since I was around, I thought I would drop off a few bottles of the shampoo I used on Boy that you mentioned you liked." He handed them to me.

"That was nice of you."

"It's not so nice. They were sample bottles. I got them for free." He shrugged.

"Well, even so, it's a nice gesture. Thank you."

Sebastian pointed to the old sheet rock near the trash cans. "It looks like you're doing some renovation."

"Yeah, believe it or not, today was the last day for the electricity. The plumber finished up too, earlier this week. There's lots more to do before the Kensington House Bed-and-Breakfast is ready to open, but I'm looking forward to what's next."

"You should be. It's an exciting time." He stood there awkwardly for a moment before looking at his watch. "Well, I'd better get going. Enjoy the electricity. Let there be light!"

"Thanks," I said with a smile.

As Sebastian walked away, I tried to refrain from watching him go and opened the lid of the mailbox. Several envelopes were inside. I pulled them out and closed the door.

William was standing in the dining area near the window. "He seems like a nice young man. Going out of his way to deliver you shampoo." He looked at me with raised eyebrows.

"I know what you're thinking, William, but we're just friends." *At least, for now.*

William seemed unconvinced but was polite enough not to pursue the matter.

I put the shampoo down on the dining table and flipped through the envelopes in my hand. I frowned.

"What is it?" he asked.

"I don't know. Some kind of letter from an attorney." I opened it. "Ugh. Allison, Joe's sister, is contesting the inheritance."

"What does that signify?"

"She's trying to take Joe's money away from me. *And this house.*" I wasn't surprised. I knew she wouldn't leave me alone. She had the tenacity of her brother. And the vindictiveness. Like Joe, Allison had no interest in Kensington House. She just didn't want *me* to have it. "Well, I guess she's in for a fight."

"Strange," William said. "I thought you didn't believe in violence."

I glanced at William to explain that I didn't mean the word *fight* in the physical sense, but the corners of his lips curved upward. *Had William just told a joke?*

"Hopefully, your other correspondence conveys more positive news," he said.

I looked at the other envelopes in my hand. One was from the Salem Historical Society. I opened it. "Hey, it *is* good news. Our application for a plaque—you know, to place on the exterior of Kensington House to show it's a historical property—has been approved."

The corners of William's lips curved back down. "Maybe the person at the society is right. Maybe it isn't best to publicize this."

I put the letter down. "William, you're innocent. And I meant what I said. I am going to do everything in my power to prove that."

"You are kind, Clara. That reminds me." He reached up toward the framed Ground Rules that were hanging on the wall and pulled them down.

"What are you doing?" I asked.

"Making a minor adjustment."

He pulled out the sheet of paper, took a pencil that was lying on the table, and erased the last ground rule I had penciled in: *Rule Number Four: We don't talk about the past.* He replaced the framed document on the wall.

"I've resolved not to flee from my past," he said.

I glanced at the letter from Allison's lawyer. "Me too. We'll fight together. You know, in the metaphorical sense."

"Indeed."

My phone pinged. I reached for it in my pocket. "Oh, it's Anna."

"Anna?"

"She's the woman who moved into Marlena Ryder's house. She said next Tuesday was good for our first book club meeting."

"Book club?"

"Yeah, we've started our own book club. It's just the three of us, really. But that's fine with me. We're going to meet here next week for dinner and discuss our first selection. We're starting with a classic. *Anna Karenina.* By Tolstoy."

"Did you say *three*? If my math is correct, you and Anna are only two individuals."

I smiled. "Well, I'm including you, too."

William stood there, looking at me.

"Would you like to join us?" I asked. "Are you familiar with *Anna Karenina*?"

"I've read this book. Many times."

"Well, then you'll have a lot to contribute."

"But ..."

"Well, I figured you can either write down your thoughts about the book, and we—well, *I*—can share them at the meeting. Or you can comment during the meeting as Anna and I discuss the book, and I'll relay your thoughts, saying, 'My friend William said ...'"

"Your friend William?"

"Of course. I told you. You're my best friend."

Bark!

Boy came running into the dining room and sat in front of me eagerly.

"Is it dinnertime already?" I asked.

Ghost Cat walked into the room from under the stairway, as if it was dinnertime for her as well. She curled herself around a table leg and purred.

"How nice of you to join us," I said to her. "Are you here for the unveiling?"

"Unveiling?" William asked.

"This is a momentous occasion. Our first meal with electricity."

I quickly set the table for one and prepared Boy's food bowls. Then I picked up Boy and positioned myself by the light switch near the front door as, outside, the sun sank lower in the sky.

"Are you ready?" I asked William.

"Indeed."

"How about you?" I asked Boy.

Bark!

"And you?" I asked Ghost Cat, who was rubbing her head against the table leg and totally ignoring me.

"Works for me! Okay, here we go ... one, two, three!"

I flipped the wall switch, and as light spilled across the room for the first time in I didn't know how many years, William Kensington broke into a wide smile.

In my heart of hearts, I hoped it was the first of many smiles in this glorious old house.

The story of Clara and William continues! Get *Here Ghost Nothing*, Book 3 in the Salem Spirits Cozy Mysteries series, and join them on their next haunted adventure!

Sign up for Dina Marie's email newsletter and get a Salem Spirits Cozy Mysteries short story for free! Yes, free! Visit dinamariebooks.com for details.

About the Author

DINA MARIE IS THE pen name of award-winning novelist Dina Santorelli, who has been obsessed with all things ghost since . . . well, forever. Married on Halloween, she likes vacationing in spooky cities and visiting cemeteries and haunted hotels. A recent visit to Salem, Massachusetts, inspired her Salem Spirits series, which she wrote, in part, for her mom, a lover of cozy mystery TV.